A ROGUE COWBOY'S CHRISTMAS SURPRISE

A Hart Ranch Billionaire's Novel

STEPHANIE ROWE

COPYRIGHT

For my beta readers, who went above and beyond on this one.
THANK YOU! I couldn't do this without you!

ACKNOWLEDGMENTS

Special thanks to my beta readers. You guys are the best!

There are so many to thank by name, more than I could count, but here are those who I want to called out specially for all they did to help this book come to life: Alyssa Bird, Ashlee Murphy, Bridget Koan, Britannia Hill, Deb Julienne, Denise Fluhr, Dottie Jones, Heidi Hoffman, Helen Loyal, Jackie Moore Kranz, Jean Bowden, Jeanne Stone, Jeanie Jackson, Jodi Moore, Judi Pflughoeft, Kasey Richardson, Linda Watson, Regina Thomas, Summer Steelman, Suzanne Mayer, Shell Bryce, and Trish Douglas. Special thanks to my family, who I love with every fiber of my heart and soul. And to AER, who is my world. Love you so much, baby girl! And to Joe, who keeps me believing myself. I love you all! And special love to my favorite mom! You're the best ever!

ABOUT THE BOOK

Romance bookstore owner Sofia Navarro never forgot the homeless, handsome stranger who risked his life to save hers so long ago.

Billionaire cowboy Keegan Hart, aka rescue dog dad, never forgot Sofia's sass, her spirit, her warmth, or the way she opened the heart of the rebellious loner who had lost everything.

Neither of them forgot the intense, passionate love affair that ended too soon. He has tried to find her, but the fake name she gave him made it impossible.

And now, seventeen years later, they're about to get brought together again...by a secret that Sofia has kept from him since that day. A secret that will change his life forever. A secret that puts her in great danger. A secret that will no longer be contained.

But Christmas is a time for miracles, magic, and mistletoe,

and the surprises that can heal hearts that have been broken for a very long time.

ABOUT THE AUTHOR: *New York Times* and *USA Today* bestselling author Stephanie Rowe is the author of more than fifty novels. Stephanie is Vivian® Award nominee, a RITA® Award winner and five-time nominee, and a Golden Heart® Award winner and two-time nominee.

CHAPTER ONE

KEEGAN HART BRACED his hands on his kitchen counter and bowed his head, swearing under his breath. "Dead?"

His brother, Brody Hart, nodded. "I'm sorry to tell you. That's why it's been so difficult to track Sascha."

Keegan swore under his breath. Sascha Rose shouldn't matter to him. He had known her for a brief time long ago, but he'd never forgotten her. He looked over at his brother, who had slogged through the sleet and ice to deliver it in person. "How did she die?"

"Car accident. Off a cliff."

He stared at his brother. "Car accident? Off a cliff? That's like a movie. Who drives off a cliff?" It didn't even make sense. She'd been so full of vitality and life. "When?"

"Fifteen years ago."

Keegan ran his hand through his hair and let out his breath. "All this time you've been looking for her, and she's been dead?"

"Yeah." Brody grimaced.

"How did it take that long to find her? Wasn't it in the papers? Certificates of death aren't difficult to find." Fifteen years. Sascha had been dead for *fifteen* years. His mind was whirling.

"See, that's the thing. Her name wasn't really Sascha Rose."

Keegan stared at his brother. "She lied to me about her name?" That actually made sense. It didn't surprise him, and it somehow made some of the tension ease.

"Yeah." Brody slid a paper across the table. "Her real name was Sofia Pendleton."

Keegan took the paper and looked at it. The moment he saw her face, his gut tightened. "It's her."

"Yeah."

He traced his finger over her jaw. In the photograph, she couldn't have been much older than when he knew her. She was laughing in the photograph, her eyes sparkling with mischief, behind her studious glasses. He smiled. "I remember that smile."

"This is her obituary picture." Brody put another photograph on the counter.

This time, Keegan frowned. Sascha had her hair in a tight bun. She was wearing a navy sweater, and she wasn't smiling. Contact lenses gave a clear view of her eyes, and Keegan saw the pain in them that she'd tried to hide, that he'd seen only once, that last night, before everything fell apart. "She wasn't happy when that picture was taken." Dammit. He'd always imagined she'd gone off to a brilliant, vibrant life.

"One more thing—" Brody stopped.

Alarm settled in Keegan's gut as he looked sharply at his brother. "What's wrong?"

"I don't know how to tell you this..."

"What?"

"She had a kid with her in the car. A daughter. She was fifteen months old at the time she died."

"A baby?" Keegan looked at the date of death, the age of

the toddler at that time, then did the math. The timing matched his week with Sascha. Keegan sank down on the bar stool, the Christmas baking forgotten. "You don't think—"

"That the baby was yours? Sofia was married at the time she died. If she met him right after you, the baby could have been his."

"We were intimate one night. What are the odds?"

"Not that high."

He met Brody's gaze. "But not zero."

"Nope."

"Can you find any more info about the baby?"

"Sofia wasn't married at the time she gave birth, but they married shortly afterwards. This is the only photograph I found of the baby, at the christening." He slid another photograph across the counter.

Keegan took the picture. Sascha was right in the middle of a group of people all fancied up. In her arms was a little baby, but it was impossible to tell much about what the baby looked like. Beside her stood a man who, according to the caption, was her husband. "What about her husband? Good guy?"

Brody shrugged. "Seemed fine. He remarried and has some kids. Rich finance guy with all the right connections."

"So, maybe she was happy before she died." He picked up the photograph of the obituary photo again, and saw the pain in her eyes. She wasn't happy. Not in that photograph. "It doesn't matter. It was a long time ago."

Brody laughed softly. "I'm your brother. Don't waste your time lying to me. I know. I always know."

Keegan took a breath, then shrugged his shoulders. "Let's set up a fund in the name of her and her daughter."

"Sure. What do you want to fund?"

Keegan thought for a moment, but came up with nothing.

He didn't know Sascha well enough to know what would have mattered to her. "I don't know."

Brody nodded. "Well, think about it. You'll figure it out." He set a folder on the counter. "That's the rest of the info I have. It's pretty sparse, but maybe you'll find it interesting."

"Yeah. Thanks." Keegan didn't pick up the folder. "Maybe later. I need to get back to work."

Brody looked around at the kitchen, where the ingredients for pumpkin bread were spread across every surface. "Still working on that new pumpkin bread recipe?"

"Yeah." Every year, Keegan created a new recipe for his local customers, the ones who had stood beside him all those years ago, before he opened his business. When he was baking for fun. They always got a special treat a year before he introduced it to his bakery.

Brody raised his brows. "Christmas is a week away."

"I know. I'll get it. Bella said she'd help me brainstorm."

Bella was one of their sisters, and she owned the café that was on the half of their property that was a high-end dude ranch vacation destination. The other half was a ranch for rescued horses. Keegan often provided the desserts for her restaurant, and she was key in brainstorming new recipes for the bakery.

Brody nodded. "I need to get back to the ranch. The roads are sheer ice right now. Is Bella walking over?"

Keegan raised his brows. "She's almost thirty years old, Brody. I don't keep track of how she's getting to my house."

Brody grinned. "I'll never stop protecting my family, so don't bother trying to talk me out of it."

"I know." Keegan was suddenly restless, wanting to focus on the baking, and not the memories staring up at him from the folder Brody had handed him. "Look, I need to get back to work."

Brody nodded. "You okay?"

4

"Sure. It was a long time ago." A long time ago, yes, but at the same time, it felt like yesterday. And he couldn't stop thinking about her daughter. Was she his? Had he had a kid, and he never knew it? The loss was staggering, even though he didn't know if it was true.

"All right." Brody rocked forward against the counter, as if he were going to say something else, but then shrugged. "Call if you want to talk about it."

"I won't. I'm fine." Keegan grabbed a potholder and opened the oven. "Say hey to Tatum for me." Brody's new wife was a shining light in the Hart family. She made his brother happy, and gave them all hope that at least one of them had found love.

"Will do."

Keegan didn't look over at his brother, concentrating on starting a fresh batch of batter.

Brody waited for a moment, and then turned to leave. He'd just put his hand on the door, when Keegan stopped him. "What was her name?"

"Who?"

"Sascha's daughter."

"Gabriella. Gabriella Holland. That was Sascha's married name. Sofia Pendleton Holland."

Gabriella Holland. Sofia Holland. The names meant nothing to him, but the photograph hadn't lied. "Thanks."

"You bet. Dinner this weekend?"

"Of course." Every Sunday, all the Harts who were in town gathered at one of their houses for dinner. They all had houses on the ranch. They were often joined by a Stockton or two, which was the family one of their sisters had married into. The Stocktons were a good bunch, and the families were already close.

"All right." Brody bumped his fist lightly against the door, then turned and left.

The minute the door closed behind him, Keegan sat down again and pressed his hands to his forehead. Sascha was dead. All this time, she'd been dead. And her daughter...

He picked up the christening photograph again and studied it, but it was too grainy to see if the baby had his eyes or jaw or anything that looked like him.

Not that it mattered. That had all ended fifteen years ago, and what might have been was long since past.

CHAPTER TWO

"Mom! Wake up! Mom!"

Sofia Navarro bolted awake, jolted to alertness by her daughter's urgent whisper. "What is it?"

Her first thought was that *he* had found them, and she started reaching for the nightstand, for the gun she still kept there, even after all these years. Instead of the gun, her hand hit the stuffed Santa Claus and knocked it to the floor. "What's wrong?"

"It's midnight. It's time." Gabby was leaning over her, her dark eyes shadowed in the night.

Sofia stared at her daughter, her tension easing at the expression on her daughter's face. Whatever it was, it wasn't life threatening. With a sigh of relief, Sofia propped herself up on her elbows, trying to catch up to what was happening. "It's time for what? Christmas isn't for a week, so no presents yet."

"To tell me who my dad is."

Sudden alarm gripped her. "What?"

Gabby sat down on the bed. "You always said that when I

was sixteen, you'd tell me who my dad was. As of five seconds ago, I'm sixteen. So it's time."

Sofia flopped back on the bed and put her pillow over her face. "I told you that when you were ten years old."

"I have a memory like a steel trap." Gabby poked Sofia's hip. "It's time."

Sofia pulled the pillow down and studied her daughter. Sofia's long, dark hair was pulled forward over one shoulder, and her olive skin was luminous in the dim light. God, she loved her kid. "Happy birthday, baby girl. Do you want your present? It's an heirloom I've been holding onto for you since you were born—"

"Mom. I want to know who my dad is."

"You're irritatingly persistent."

Gabby grinned. "I learned it from you, Mom. I wouldn't be a good daughter if I didn't make you follow through on the promises you didn't actually mean when you said them."

Sofia wrinkled her nose. "Deep dark secrets are usually best left alone."

"How can it be dark? It created me, and I'm sparkly sunshine, right?"

"You are very sparkly," Sofia agreed as she leaned over and turned on the bedside lamp. They both blinked at the sudden light. Her room was filled with Christmas decorations, a season she always loved, but right now, those good feelings were hidden in a sea of "uh, oh." "Knowing his name won't change anything. You're perfect and beautiful exactly as you are."

Gabby let out a sigh. "Mom, you've drilled my self-worth into me since I was born. I get that I don't need a dad. But I deserve to know who he is." She shrugged. "Even if he's a serial killer, it's okay. I'm fine with that. I just want to know."

"He's not a serial killer."

"Great. Then it's all good." Gabby gestured with her hand. "Let it all out. It's time."

Sofia grabbed her glasses from the nightstand and put the bright blue frames on. Her daughter's face came into perfect focus, and she saw the desperation in Gabby's eyes. Desperate, urgent longing that was almost painful.

She sighed, realizing that, despite her best efforts to brainwash Gabby about the irrelevance of dads everywhere, the teenager had developed her own opinion. Teenagers, right? "Gabriella, he doesn't know you exist."

Gabby rolled her eyes. "You told me that already. Repeatedly. Trust me, I know that."

"It's just a name."

"It's not just a name. It's my *identity*." Gabby held up her hand. "I know, I know. Who my biological dad is doesn't impact who I am, but it's like this big black hole. I just need to fill in the pieces. I need that."

The urgency in Gabby's voice was clear. She *needed* to know.

Damn. Sofia was going to have to tell her daughter the truth.

The second Sofia thought it, her heart started pounding. How would Gabby react? Oh, boy. "You have to promise me you won't try to contact him."

Gabby's eyes widened. "He's still alive?"

There was far too much eagerness in Gabby's face, and apprehension crept down Sofia's spine. "You have to promise."

"I don't have to promise. You already promised you'd tell me, without any conditions. You can't change it now."

The most important thing that Sofia had always stressed with her daughter was the importance of trust and honesty. If she broke her promise to tell Gabby, her daughter would never trust her again.

"Why doesn't he know I exist?" Gabby prompted, clearly trying to get the ball rolling. "Why didn't you tell him?"

"Sweetheart. I doubt he would even remember me." She could only hope. It had been only a few days, but the intensity had etched itself into her soul forever. Maybe he'd forgotten. Or maybe not.

"Was it a one-night stand?" Gabby asked.

Sofia kicked back the covers and stood up, pacing across the room in her fuzzy snowman socks. "No. Not really."

"What does that mean?"

Sofia turned toward her daughter. "I was eighteen. I'd actually...run away." She paused, trying to figure out how to tell the story without giving away the things she didn't want her daughter burdened with.

"Really? You?" Gabby was clearly surprised to hear that her responsible mom had been such a wild child.

If only she knew.

Sofia nodded as she grabbed her robe and wrapped it around herself, trying to feel safe. "I was supposed to be driving cross country to go to college, but that was my mom's dream, not mine. I decided to stop in Portland and do my life the way I wanted."

Gabby wrapped her arms around her knees. "I can't believe you were a rebel."

"I know, right? I'm so old and boring now."

"Totally. Keep going."

"Right. Well, it was about two in the morning. The city was dark, and I'd gotten myself lost. I stepped right out in front of a truck without looking. The horn honked, and I froze. I would have died, but then a boy ran out of an alley and literally tackled me out of the way."

Gabby's mouth opened. "He saved your life?"

"Yep."

"My dad risked his own life to save yours?"

"Yep."

Gabby grinned. "Cool."

Sofia clasped her hands on her head, remembering that moment, that day. "He was homeless, living under a bridge with a bunch of other kids. He had no family, no rules, no obligations. I loved it. He was this representation of who I wanted to be and what I wanted."

Gabby leaned forward. "Was he hot?"

Sofia smiled. "Not in the traditional sense. He was kind of rough, but there was a kindness to him that I loved. He lived a life of freedom, and I burned for that. I spent the next few days hanging out with him. He showed me around the city, a different side of life."

Gabby frowned. "It wasn't a hot and heavy sex thing?"

Oh, God. "No, it wasn't. We were just friends. It was nice."

"Nice? That's it? *Nice*? How did it go from nice to getting naked?"

"Naked?" Sofia raised her brows. It had been so much more than "nice." But not nakedness, not until the end.

Gabby held out her hands innocently. "Since I exist, I'm making the assumption that it went from nice and friendly to naked. No?"

Sofia couldn't tell the rest of the story. She couldn't possibly explain to her daughter what had happened. She still ached in her heart for how it had ended so quickly and so terribly between them. Of what that one night had unleashed in her life over the next few years, until she'd run for her life and her daughter's in the middle of the night, praying that they'd never be found again.

No. She wasn't going back there. She'd made it out, she had her awesome kid, and her career was a gift that took care of them and kept them safe. "Gabriella, I will never regret what happened with him or afterwards, because it gave you to me."

Gabby's face softened. "Mom, I know that. I love you, too. What happened next?"

Sofia took a breath. She couldn't admit to her daughter what had happened next. But she hadn't promised the entire story. She'd promised only one thing. A name. "The homeless kids he lived with, under the bridge, all took the same last name. They created a family."

Gabby sucked in her breath, her eyes wide with anticipation. "What name?"

"Hart."

"Hart," she repeated. "Hart?"

"Yes." Sofia waited for a heartbeat. Then a second one.

Gabby suddenly bolted to her feet. "*Hart*? As in the tech geniuses who sold their company for billions? The ones who are always in the press because they're rich as hell? And now they own a massive horse ranch in Eastern Oregon? My dad is one of *those* Harts?" She didn't wait for Sofia to answer. "It *is* those Harts, isn't it? I remember now that they were homeless kids living under a bridge. Every article about them mentions their story. Holy crap, Mom! My dad's a Hart! He's a freaking billionaire!"

"Yep." Sofia's chest tightened. "Gabby, don't forget what I said. I doubt he even remembers me. So many people try to get into his life because he's a rich celebrity. There's no way he'd remember me, or believe you—"

"Which Hart?" Gabby interrupted. "Brody? The one who just married the country music star, Tatum Crosby? Or Dylan, that private detective? Or Colin, that smoke jumper? Which one? Mom, which one's my dad?"

Sofia let out her breath, the name sticking in her throat. It was a secret she'd held for sixteen years, for so many good reasons.

"Mom?"

As soon as she spoke it, she would be unleashing Pandora's Box. She tried one last time. "Are you sure you want to know?"

"Mom!"

She closed her eyes, took a deep breath, and then spoke the name she'd held in secret for so long. "Keegan," she said softly. "Keegan Hart is your biological father."

CHAPTER THREE

KEEGAN SAT down on the floor across from his new dog, who was sitting on the armchair he'd dragged into the kitchen for her. "I have a question."

The eight-pound shaggy rescue cocked her head at him.

"You didn't eat the pumpkin bread. Are you just not a pumpkin fan? Or is it so bad that even a dog who has lived on the streets won't touch it?"

The dog, who he was contemplating calling Millie, thumped her freshly washed tail at him, clearly not wanting to crush his soul.

He sighed. He'd been working on the recipe for weeks, and he couldn't get it right. He was tired of working on it and getting nowhere.

Baking had once been his joy, but now that he'd finally opened the bakery he'd dreamed of, the magic was gone.

"On the plus side," he told his dog. "Your tail is impressive. We owe my little sisters for my skills that got those mats out." As kids, he'd been the brother to help the girls untangle their hair when things got too difficult.

Millie's tail looked good. Fluffy and speckled. More than

he would have expected based on Millie's state when he'd first plucked her out of the alley yesterday.

He'd spent the last twenty-four hours cleaning up and checking out the little dog who had been hanging around the Hart Family Youth Center for over a week. He had staff who did deliveries nowadays, or he would have heard about the dog earlier.

As it was, he'd popped over to put in an appearance at the annual Christmas party and spotted Millie on his way out. The minute he saw her little black face peeking around the dumpster, hoping the kids would toss some food her way, he'd decided she was his.

He'd never had a dog before, but he had horses galore on the ranch, so he figured it would work fine.

Millie had been trickier than he'd expected: scared, scrawny, and she had no idea how to live in a house. Stairs? Beds? Enough food that she didn't have to scarf it down frantically for fear it would disappear before she could eat it? Housebreaking? All new.

Kinda reminded him of himself, back in the day.

Waiting for his next question, Millie panted at him, not used to living in a building that wasn't sub-zero temps.

Another thing he could relate to from his teenage years.

Twenty-four hours was all the time he'd had to get Millie acclimated before he'd had to get back to work. He'd stumbled across her the day after Brody had told him about Sascha, and he'd latched onto the chance to distract himself from memories by saving the dog.

She'd definitely distracted him, but she hadn't yet helped him figure out the Christmas recipe that was eluding him.

"What do you think it needs? Maybe I'll toss some spinach in there? Or grapefruit?" Hell, he might as well. Nothing he'd tried so far had worked.

She wagged her little tail and offered no guidance.

Keegan leaned his head back against the polished cabinet and bumped it gently. "I gotta warn you, Millie, I'm not in a great place right now. Feel free to bite me if I start to drag you down."

Millie jumped off the chair, then bounded over to him and hopped in his lap. He laughed softly as she put her paws on his chest and licked his cheek, wagging her little body.

He grinned and put his hand on her side, frowning when he felt her ribs sticking out.

He knew about that, too. Being homeless had been rough as hell, until he'd found Brody and the others. "Look," he said. "I don't know how you ended up on the street, but in this family, we take care of each other. Even if something happens to me, one of my brothers or sisters will step in." Millie pulled back and stared up at him, her huge brown eyes fixed on his. "You're safe now, Millie. I promise."

Just as how Brody had made that promise to Keegan when he'd found him shivering in that alley so long ago. *You're safe now.* "You are," he said as he ruffled her head. "I promise."

She licked his chin, making him grin. "Less than twenty-four hours, and you're turning me into a dog person. Never thought that I'd go for anything other than horses, but you win."

It was amazing how a little shaggy creature could make his huge house feel so much fuller so quickly.

"Keegan? Where are you? Who are you talking to?" His sister Bella's voice drifted in from the front hall.

Millie bolted off his lap and dove under the armchair, disappearing out of sight behind the flap on the bottom.

Right. Life on the streets had made her not trust people. He got that, too. Sascha was the only person he'd trusted, until she'd—

No. He wasn't going there again. "Down here." He

stretched out his legs, and then stood up as Bella walked into the kitchen.

His sister was wearing jeans, a red Santa hat, and a sweatshirt with the grinch on it. She frowned. "Why were you on the floor?"

"It's a nice floor."

She put her hands on her hips. "Dammit. I knew you weren't doing well, but I didn't think you were to the point of laying on the floor in the middle of baking. Keegan, what's going on with you? Seriously." She tossed her bag on the table and sat down on one of the bar stools. "I'm not helping you bake until you talk to me."

He turned off the oven, giving up for now. "Aren't you going to ask me why there's an armchair in the kitchen?"

Bella glanced around, then her eyes widened. "You've lost your mind, I'm guessing. It happens with a traumatic childhood, you know. I mean, we all thought you were the one who was going to be okay, but—"

At that moment, Millie poked her nose out from under the chair and wiggled it, clearly trying to catch a whiff of Bella.

His sister's mouth dropped open. "You got a *dog?*"

"Yeah. She was homeless, hanging around the Youth Center."

Her face softened in understanding. "Homeless?"

"Yep. Skinny. Scared," Keegan said.

Bella smiled. "What else to do but make her family, then?"

"Right?" Of course Bella would understand. "She said the pumpkin bread sucks."

Bella frowned. "It can't suck. You're a great baker."

Silently, he slid a plate across the granite counter toward her.

She took a bite, then wrinkled her nose. "Well, it doesn't

suck, but there's nothing special about it, not like what you usually create."

"I know." He watched the chair as Millie stuck her nose a little bit further out. "I think I'm going to cancel the product release. I'm running out of time."

Bella sighed. "You always give your local customers a special product every year. They treasure it. You promised them and yourself that you'd keep doing that even after you opened the commercial bakery."

"I know." He'd been servicing small local businesses exclusively for years until he'd finally decided to open a commercial bakery. Business for the bakery had been great, but it wasn't working for him on an emotional level. "I got nothing, Bella. I don't know if I can keep going with the bakery."

Bella sat down. "This has been your dream since we were kids."

"I know." He shrugged. "I don't know. Maybe you can take a look at the recipe? See if you see anything?" Bella owned a café on the guest portion of the ranch, and the two of them spent plenty of time in the kitchen experimenting together. He pushed the computer over to her.

"Sure. We got this." She opened the computer and typed in his password. "Who's that?"

"What?" He glanced at the computer, then grimaced when he saw what she was looking at. "Sascha."

"*Sascha?*" Bella stared at him. "You're still looking at the photobooth shot from when you were eighteen? With a girl you knew for a week and never heard from again? Why?"

The series of photos from the photobooth was open on the left side of his screen. "Long story."

Bella folded her arms over her chest. "I have nowhere to go. Tell me."

Keegan didn't feel like talking about it, especially the fact that Sascha was dead and it was bugging him more than he would have expected, but the Harts had a family rule that you didn't keep secrets from each other. It was how they'd survived their time under the bridge. So, he gave a truth, but a different one. "Because of the joy."

"The joy?"

He nodded. "Look how hard we're laughing. At that time, we were both broke and homeless. We had nothing, or at least I didn't. I don't know her whole story. I had *nothing* back then, and I was so freaking happy in that picture."

"So, you're longing for this girl you knew for a week?"

"No. It's inspiration, Bella. Sascha was pure positive energy. I've never met anyone else with such a passion for being alive." He rested his forearms on the counter. "I never told any of you this, but back then, I was thinking about killing myself. After I lost my mom and wound up on the streets, even Brody couldn't help me get my emotions under control—"

"What?" Bella looked shocked. "You carried that all alone? How did we not know this?"

"Yeah, well, it took me a while to warm up to everyone. And then I met Sascha. She lit up my world, and she made me see life in a different light. She changed me forever." Sascha had simply swept into his life for a week and then swept back out, equally as quickly, but she'd left her mark. "She showed me how to love life no matter what. She was... electric." It was the best word he could think of, but it still didn't do justice to her.

Bella studied the photos. "And you're trying to feel that energy again? That's why you have it up?"

"Yeah." He shrugged. "We have everything we could ever want, Bella. We're rich as sin, can do whatever we want whenever we want, donate to charities all day long, and I still don't feel as alive as I did back then."

Bella sighed. "You know, I hate to say it, but I get that.

I feel the same way sometimes." She leaned back. "There was something about living under the bridge, huddled together for warmth. It was the first time in my life I felt safe, which is crazy, since we were living under a freaking bridge."

"Not me. That bridge life was tough for me." Keegan watched Millie's nose wiggling as she sniffed. "I was happy before my mom died. We'd had a house. A home. Laughter. Love. Even Brody and you guys couldn't fill that void. Nothing could."

"Until Sascha."

He nodded. "Sounds stupid, right? I mean, she was like a breeze that was gone before she even touched down." That described Sascha exactly. A breeze that could sweep others up in her power, but never slowed and never touched down.

"All right. Let's channel Breezy Sascha and get this recipe together." Bella leaned in to look at the recipe. "And then you can help me figure out this new chicken dish, because I've lost my muse, too, big brother."

"It's a deal—" At that moment, his phone rang. He glanced at it, and saw it was Sadie, who was in charge of all the logistics at the bakery. He gestured at Bella that he was taking the call, then put the call on speaker while he began to organize his ingredients. "What's up, Sadie?"

"The driver who was supposed to take the Local C Route has a family emergency, and she's out for the next three days. I don't have anyone to take the route."

Keegan swore. "We have to deliver to them. Switch someone else to that route."

"Everyone has already left. I'd drive, but I need to stay here and keep things moving."

Bella looked over. "What's the Local C route?"

"It's a route that delivers to a bunch of my original customers. The mom-and-pop markets who sold Hart Bakery

items when there wasn't a Hart Bakery. They're top priority."
He rubbed his jaw. "Maybe we can get—"

"Us," Bella interrupted suddenly. "Let's do the delivery.
You and me. Get out there, remember why we do this.
Remember the people who matter to us."

Keegan frowned at her. "I need to get this recipe done,
and I don't want to leave Millie—"

"Bring Millie, and we can work on the way. You're not
making any progress anyway." Bella clapped her hands
together excitedly. "This feels right, Keegan. Let's do it. You
need it. I need it. It's a gift. Let's take it."

Keegan looked around his kitchen. Ingredients were
everywhere. Pumpkin bread was on multiple plates, all of it
subpar. In the past, the scene would have ignited a spark of
excitement in him. Today? It was a place he didn't want to be.

"Keegan?" Sadie asked. "What do you want to do?"

Decision made. He needed to get out of there. "I'll take
the route, Sadie. Bella and I. We'll be there in ten minutes."

"It's an overnight route—"

"That's fine. We'll pack fast." He hung up and grinned at
his sister. "You're crazy."

"I know! Yay! Road trip! I'll meet you at the warehouse!"
She grabbed her bag and ran for the door, while Keegan
dropped to his stomach and stretched out on the floor in
front of the chair.

"Mille."

She poked her head out and pricked her ears.

"Want to go on a road trip?"

Her head began to wiggle as the force of her tail wag
made her entire body move. She belly crawled out from under
the chair and pressed her cold nose against his, her brown
eyes fixed on his.

Keegan didn't have time to run around delivering food.
He didn't have time for a dog.

But he was also done with waking up every morning and feeling empty, unable to appreciate the life he had.

So, he was going...and keeping the dog.

CHAPTER FOUR

"GIRL, you are one badass bitch, and I never knew it!"

Sofia felt her cheeks heat up as she shoved a box of newly arrived romance novels into the arms of her best friend and business partner, Jocie Wilson. "You always knew I was a badass bitch."

"But not when it came to sex! Keegan Hart? Seriously? Millions of women would sacrifice their first born to get in his pants, and you *got* your first born by getting into his pants. The irony is not lost on me, sweetheart."

Jocie started laughing. "He wasn't the Keegan Hart everyone wants back then. He was the Keegan Hart no one wanted."

"Except you, because you clearly are a visionary woman." Jocie put the box down on the floor with a thump and pointed to the easy chairs that they had nestled around the fireplace, encouraging customers to settle down with a coffee, a pastry, and a newly purchased book to enjoy themselves. "Case in point, the amazing circle of readers you have created in our store."

Sofia smiled. "They are great, aren't they?" Right now, there were Christmas stockings hanging on the fireplace, strands of white lights twinkling all over the store, and signs promising a visit from Santa Claus on Sunday afternoon.

"They are, but we're not opening the store on time today. We're going to sit down, drink lattes, and you're finally going to tell me all the raunchy details that you've kept hidden for so long."

"The details are top secret. I'm already regretting telling you why Gabby refused to come down to help out this morning." On Saturdays, Gabby ran the register in their little bookstore/coffee shop that specialized in romance novels. *Happily Ever After Again* had been a dream that had fallen into their lap when Sofia's landlord had told her that she was going to put the building on the market.

A week later, after taking out loans they barely afford, Sofia and Jocie had purchased the building with its little store downstairs and two-bedroom apartment upstairs and decided to give access to the dream of happily ever after to every woman in the western Seattle suburbs.

Eleven years later, *Happily Ever After Again* hosted eleven book clubs, bridge night, a knitting circle, many visiting authors, and an annual Christmas party that included a gift tree for the local women's shelter much like the ones where Sofia had spent much of her childhood with her mom.

"I don't blame Gabby for being mad," Jocie said, as she headed over to the coffee nook and began to brew them up some caffeine. "If I was sixteen and found out my mom had been holding out on a Keegan Hart dad for me, I'd be pissed, too. She probably spent the rest of the night making lists of all the expensive things she could have had if he'd been paying for her upbringing."

"Probably. I definitely shorted her by not buying her a Scottish castle on her fifth birthday." Sofia walked over and flipped the sign on the door to "Open." "She was pretty mad I hadn't given Keegan the chance to decide to be a part of her life."

Gabby had texted at five this morning, telling Sofia she wasn't coming to breakfast and banning her from bothering her. Sofia had knocked on the door a few times, but Gabby had refused to answer.

It was unlike Gabby to get that mad, and Sofia wasn't sure if the best response was to give her space, or force her to talk it out. So far, Sofia was giving her space, but eventually, she'd have to go in there.

Jocie hit the button on the latte machine and then turned to Sofia, folding her arms across her chest. Her dark skin was radiant in the morning light, making Sofia's olive skin almost look pale. "Let's go over that one, girl. What exactly made you decide not to tell him? From what I hear, he would have paid up. That family is a little obsessed with funding things for kids, to make sure that no kids are left without resources like they were."

"I didn't want his money."

"Really? You don't want child support from a billionaire who is your daughter's biological dad? That makes total sense. What single mom would want that kind of cash?"

Sofia glanced at her best friend. "If I told him, then I'd be trapped."

Jocie met her gaze, and understanding flickered in them. "Maybe he's a good guy," she said softly. "Maybe he's not like your ex was."

Sofia shrugged. "Back then, I had no idea who Keegan was. I didn't know if I could trust him," she said. "He was a homeless rebel. And then I met my ex-husband and...things are different now."

"But now—"

"What if Keegan's not a nice guy? If I told him, then he'd

have control over Gabby and me for the rest of our lives." The thought made a chill shiver down her spine. "I can't ever give up my freedom, Jocie. Not for any amount of money."

Jocie inclined her head. "I get that. I do. But he's been in the press a lot. Nothing bad is ever written about him."

"The Harts have the money to buy off the press, and we both know it."

"The press is pretty relentless. If he were a serial killer, they'd probably have figured it out by now."

Sofia couldn't help but laugh. "I don't think he's a serial killer."

"So, then—"

Sofia held up her hand. "It's been sixteen years, Jocie. It's over. Let it go." She turned her back on her friend and began to unpack the Christmas cookies that had arrived. Her hands stilled when she saw the label on the box. "You ordered these from Hart's Bakery?"

"They're the best around, and they give discounts to small businesses."

Sofia traced her finger over the logo that had a horse intertwined with the letters H and B. "Keegan owns the bakery. He told me about that dream. How his only memories of his mom had been baking with her. It was all he had of his childhood before he lost everything. Baking felt like home to him, and that was the one thing that he hated about living under the bridge: that he didn't have a kitchen." She tapped her finger on the table. "You made it, Keegan," she whispered. "Good for you."

She became aware of sudden silence in the store, and she looked up to find Jocie watching her with a surprised expression on her face. "What?"

"You loved him."

Sofia cleared her throat, and got busy setting out the

cookies. "I knew him for a week when I was eighteen. That's not love."

"Sure it is. It's a different love than what we'd have now, but it's love."

Sofia rolled her eyes. "Honestly, life isn't a romance novel, Jocie. You're way too romantic."

"There's no such thing as being too romantic." Jocie put the coffee cup on a cute saucer and held it out. "Let's caffeinate and talk. I need the details."

Sofia took the drink. "I'm not talking about it."

"Why not? You know I'm good to hold a secret, and that truth had to have been weighing on you like a freaking hippo on a chocolate binge. Plus, now that Gabby knows, you can't hide it away anymore. Time to face it, babe, with your best friend at your side."

Sofia paused and looked over at Jocie. There were things she'd never even told Jocie. Things she could never tell her. "It ended badly with Keegan," she said simply. "Like really ugly. Neither of us ever would want to go back there. So, it is what it is."

"Oh...so you're afraid of being rejected by him, then?"

Sofia started laughing. "Honestly, Jocie, do you ever give up?"

"Never. You know that." Jocie grinned back. "Tell you what. I'll go get the new boxes of books out of your car, and when I come back, you can tell me one thing. Cool?"

"No—"

"Can't hear you!" Jocie raced outside, and the door slammed shut behind her.

Sofia chuckled as she picked up the box of books that Jocie had dropped. As always, Jocie had made her feel better. How bad could life be when she owned a bookstore/café for romance novels, had a great kid, and a best friend who knew how to make her laugh? Everything would be fine. Gabby was a good kid. She'd adjust—

"Hey!" Jocie flung the door open. "I have bad news."

Sofia set the box down on one of the coffee tables and pulled out her pocketknife to cut the tape. "What's that? Keegan's married?"

"No. Your car's gone."

Sofia looked up. "What?"

"Yep. I'm guessing it got towed, stolen, or your lovely, sweet munchkin of a daughter took it and is driving over to meet her bio dad even as we speak. I'm going with option three, personally, given that this is a charming little town not known for its car thefts."

Sofia stared at her. "Gabby wouldn't steal my car."

"Of course she would. She's sixteen, has her license, and just found out her bio dad is a hot, rich celebrity billionaire. I'd go if I were her. You would, too. She probably left early morning, when she texted you not to come in her room. She's probably almost there by now."

"Crap!" Sofia pulled out her phone and quickly opened the Find Friends app. It circled for a minute, and Jocie leaned over her shoulder to watch. After a moment, Gabby's location came up.

Sofia's gut sank. "She's in the Cascade Mountains, only a couple hours from the Hart Ranch."

"Holy crap," Jocie said. "I'm so impressed that she did that. I love that spunk."

"Seriously?" Dear God. Sofia immediately called Gabby, but her daughter didn't answer. "Shit!" She texted her. *Gabby. Don't go after him. Call me now.*

No response.

"Dammit!" Sofia tried to call again, but this time, it went directly to voicemail. Grimly, she checked the app again, but now there was no location. "She shut her phone off." She should have broken her promise to her daughter. Dammit. "I need to call the police—"

Jocie took the phone out of her hand. "You can't."

"But—"

Jocie shook her head, all amusement gone from her face. "Keegan's a celebrity. If you get the cops involved, you risk the press. And if the press gets wind of it—"

"*He* could find us."

Jocie nodded. "He could find you."

For fifteen years, Sofia had stayed off the radar. Then one truth to her daughter, and everything was at risk.

"Can you call Keegan? Give the billionaire cowboy a heads up that his secret baby is minutes away from claiming her inheritance?" Jocie grinned. "That's literally a romance novel right there. This is awesome."

"It's not awesome, and I don't have his number. He didn't even have electricity when I knew him, let alone a phone."

"Well, then, you'd best get driving." Jocie dug her keys out of her pocket. "Take my car. I'll get online and stalk him until I find his address. I'll text it to you."

"But—"

"But what? Your kid is literally about to show up on the doorstep of a man who has no idea she exists, and she's going to announce that she's his kid. I think you better haul some ass, babycakes."

"Crap. You're right." She grabbed the keys. "I'll be in touch."

"I can't wait to hear the details."

"I'll bet." Sofia started running toward the door.

"Wait!"

She spun around. "What?"

"Are you going to wear that?"

She looked down at her jeans and *Happily Ever After Again* sweatshirt. "What's wrong with it?"

"You're about to meet your baby daddy. Maybe show a little cleavage and curves? Some makeup? Maybe get a blow out?"

"I'm going to find my daughter, not win a date with a billionaire."

"Why not do both? Billionaires can be super handy to have on speed dial."

Sofia started laughing. "Why don't you come along and date him?"

"Someone's gotta run the shop. Besides, he's yours."

"He's not mine."

"Well, he was once, for seven magical days, right?"

Sofia smiled. "They were magical, until they weren't."

"Well, there you go. Change your clothes, then head out."

Sofia had a sudden urge to run up to her room and try to look cute for the man she hadn't seen in sixteen years.

Which made her equally determined not to do it.

Instead, she headed out the door. "Call me when you find his address."

"Wait!"

Sofia paused. "What now?"

"What if you have to spend the night? Toothbrush? Clothes for tomorrow? Clothes for her?"

Crap. She was right. It would take two minutes to throw some things in a backpack. Not to dress up for him. Just because she wasn't completely losing her mind. "Right." She sprinted for the stairs.

Ten minutes later, she was on her way back through the store at a run.

"Have fun," Jocie called out. "And remember that the press are always following the Harts. You can't afford a photograph to get published."

Sofia let out her breath. "I know. I'll be careful." She hugged Jocie fiercely, and then sprinted for the door, her heart already pounding as she tried once again to call her daughter.

And once again, her daughter shut her out.

Six hours was a long time for things to go terribly wrong, and that's how long it would take her to get to the outskirts of Bend, Oregon. *Stay safe, Gabby. You're my whole life.*

Then Sofia got in the car, and she was on her way.

CHAPTER FIVE

"I'm glad we switched the deliveries to your truck," Bella said as Keegan drove them along the winding road north toward Seattle. They'd been on the road for over an hour already, and they were well into the mountains. "The vans are terrible in the snow."

"Agreed." Keegan had taken one look at the icy sleet and the forecast for more of it, and he'd decided they were doing the deliveries in his pickup truck. He'd already put on chains as they headed toward the mountains, and his truck was handling the icy roads easily.

Millie was sitting between them, harnessed to the seatbelt to keep her safe. Her chin was resting on his thigh, the wind was whipping, and the trees were glistening with the icy mix. "It feels good to be out of the house."

"I agree." Bella stretched her arms above her head, her feet resting on his dashboard. She'd brought fuzzy slippers for the ride, and packed the back with blankets, fleece coats, and more warm stuff than they could possibly wear.

Which was fine. He got it. Bella had been cold a lot as a kid before she'd caught up with the Harts, and she didn't ever want to be that cold again if they slid off the road and got stranded.

They all had something.

"You think we should head back?" Bella asked. "Wait until the roads clear?"

"Nope. I need this. I need to get out of there."

"Me, too." Bella was quiet for a moment. "Keegan?"

"Yeah." He glanced at the GPS. They were about thirty minutes from their first stop, and the anticipation was building. It had been several years since he'd seen his old customers, and he was surprisingly excited to see them again.

"You think it'll happen for us?"

"What will?"

"What Brody and Tatum have. They're so happy. It feels like a normal family when I'm around them."

"There's no such thing as normal," Keegan said. "We're good."

"I know, but...I didn't really think that it would happen for any of us. I didn't think I cared. But when I see them..." She paused. "I want it, too. Do you?"

"To grow old, fat, and happy with someone?"

"Yes. Do you?"

His mind went to Sascha...and then it went to the engagement he'd ended a year ago. "No chance. I'm good with being single."

"What about Sascha?"

He laughed softly. "I knew her for a week sixteen years ago. I like the spirit she carried with her, but as for her? I didn't know her at all. For all I know, she could have turned out to be just like Naomi." His ex-fiancée hadn't been the most altruistic person, as he'd found out almost too late.

"Naomi isn't worth thinking about." Bella's tone was hard. "Don't let her ruin you for life. Not all women will try to marry you for money while continuing to have sex with their boyfriend."

"She didn't ruin me. She just showed me that I didn't need a wife." He patted the dog by his side. "I have Millie. We're good now." The little dog sighed deeply and tucked herself closer against his thigh. "See? True love already."

Bella laughed. "How can I argue against Millie? She's the sweetest."

As Bella bent down to whisper to Millie, Keegan noticed a fresh break in the icy snowbank on the opposite side of the road. He slowed the truck, trying to see over the embankment. "Does that look like fresh tire tracks?"

Bella twisted around in her seat, then she nodded. "It does. You think a car went over?"

"Everything's icy. If they didn't have chains, it would be easy to lose control." He eased the truck to the right side of the road, then swung a U-turn. "Let's make sure no one's in trouble."

"Of course." Bella was already pulling on her boots.

Neither of them hesitated as he put the truck into park, both of them leaping out as soon as his truck was stopped.

Because helping people in need was what the Harts did, and would always do.

That was how he'd met Sascha.

Dammit.

He was going to stop thinking about her. His life was now.

CHAPTER SIX

KEEGAN WALKED over to the edge and peered down the embankment, then swore. There was an old, beat-up sedan in the ditch with a crushed front end. Beside it stood a teenager in a light jacket and no hat.

She saw them and started waving her arms, shouting at them for help.

Adrenaline rushed through him. "We're coming!" he yelled down. "Is anyone hurt?"

"No! I'm alone!" she shouted back. "I'm okay."

Relief rushed through him. "Shit. She looks young to be alone. She's a kid." How was she old enough to have her license? He must be getting ancient if licensed drivers looked like babies.

"Poor thing." Bella had put on her heavy jacket, but the girl in the ditch had sneakers and leggings on. "She's going to freeze. We need to get her right now. The hill's solid ice."

"Stay with her. I got it." While Bella yelled down to the teenager, Keegan jogged off to his truck. He grabbed two harnesses from the back, then hustled to the front of the truck and cranked the winch on its grill.

He strapped in, then hooked the spare harness over his shoulder. Within moments, he was on his way down the embankment, ice trekkers on his boots, the cable hooked at his waist. It was steep and icy, and he was damned glad the teenager was all right.

He reached the bottom. "You okay, kid?"

She didn't answer. She just stared at him, her eyes wide.

He frowned as he unhooked himself from the cable. "Hello? You okay?" Shit. Had she gone into shock? "How long have you been down here?"

She still didn't answer. She just backed herself against the car, staring at him. Her hoodie was up, so it was difficult to see her face well.

Alarm crept down his spine, and he swore under his breath as he unzipped his coat. "Put this on." He held it out to her, but when she didn't move to take it, he swore. "Did you hit your head?"

She shook her head once, and then backed up as he neared.

Swearing, he stopped, holding up his hands. "I'm not going to hurt you," he said gently, using the soothing tone he took with scared horses. "My sister, Bella, is at the top of the embankment. She'll vouch for me."

The girl said nothing.

"My name's Keegan Hart," he said. "What's your name?"

His question was met with silence.

Crap. He could see she was shivering. "You don't need to tell me your name, or put on my coat," he said softly. "But it's freezing out here, and you're wet. We need to get you warm and dry." As he spoke, he set the spare harness on the hood of her car along with his coat. "Take what you want, then strap yourself in and hook yourself to the cord. Bella will pull you up."

He backed up, giving her space. He didn't like that she

was so scared of him. He didn't like that at all. What had happened to her that made her so afraid?

She still didn't move.

He swore under his breath. "You want me to get my sister instead? Would that be better?" He started moving toward the cable. "I'll go get her, but you need to get in your car until she gets down here. You're not dressed for this—"

"Wait!"

He stopped, relieved to hear her voice. "You want to come with me?"

"Yeah. Yeah, I'll come with you. Okay."

"Great." He picked up the gear, as the girl headed toward him. "Coat?"

"Okay." She didn't make eye contact with him, keeping her head down. But she accepted his coat and put it on, swallowed up by the fabric. She pulled the hood up, obscuring her face even more. "Great. Thanks." She ducked past him and headed toward the cable, but her sneakers slipped on the ice.

He caught her arm just as she pitched forward. "I've got you."

She said nothing, but she grabbed his arm fiercely, using him for balance as he helped her across the icy slope. When they reached the cable, he paused. "You want to go up alone?"

She'd basically have to be dragged up, because there was no way she'd be able to stay on her feet in sneakers, but if she wanted that space, he'd give it.

But she shook her head. "No."

"Okay." He handed her the second harness. "Strap in, kid. We'll go up together."

"All right." She was shivering visibly, but she managed to get the harness on and tightened to his satisfaction. He clipped her and himself to the cable, then signaled to Bella.

As the cable began to retract, the girl's feet slipped again. Keegan pulled her against him, using his bulk as a shield to stabilize her as he climbed. With his trekkers and Bella's help, they were up the steep embankment in a matter of moments.

As soon as they made it to the top, Bella threw a blanket over the girl and pulled a hat over her head, chatting cheerfully, using her spark to lighten the situation, as she always did.

Bella drew the girl away from Keegan as he picked up the harnesses and took care of the winch. "My name's Bella," she said. "What's yours?"

"Gabriella," the girl said. "But you can call me Gabby."

Keegan froze. *Gabriella.* That was the name of Sascha's daughter. And Gabby looked to be about the same age that Sascha's daughter would be today. What a freaking coincidence. What the hell?

"Well, great, Gabby," Bella said. "Let's call your parents, shall we? I'm sure they're worried about you."

"My phone died. I can't call her."

"I can call. What's her number? Your mom, right? That's who we're calling?"

Gabby didn't answer.

There was a long moment of silence, and Keegan met Bella's gaze. *Shit.*

Bella put her hands on Gabby's shoulders. "Are you in trouble, Gabby? Are you running away from someone? Because if you are, we can help."

Keegan waited for her answer, his gut twisted. Every Hart knew what it was like to be a teenager in trouble. A teenager without anyone to call for help. It had been a long time, but all the memories came back raw and real whenever he ran into a kid in trouble.

She didn't answer, and Keegan turned around.

Gabby was staring right at him, her eyes big and dark. Her hood was down now, and he could see her face clearly. Shock hit him right in the gut. She looked exactly like Sascha. *Exactly*.

Son of a bitch. She had the same olive skin, thick dark hair, and brown eyes. But it was more than that. Her cheeks. Her jaw. She looked exactly as he remembered Sascha from so long ago.

"Gabby," he said, his voice raw. "Who's your mom?"

She stared at him. "She said you wouldn't remember her."

Jesus. He gripped the harnesses tighter. "Who's your mom?" he asked again.

"Sofia. Sofia Navarro."

Sofia. Navarro wasn't the right last name, but the names Sofia and Gabriella matched what Brody had given him. But Sofia and Gabriella were dead. What the hell was going on? "Did she ever go by the name Sascha Rose?"

Gabby frowned. "What? No. Her name's Sofia Navarro."

He noticed her use of the present tense. "She's alive? Your mom?"

"Alive? Of course."

Alive. Was it Sascha? Was that even possible? His heart started racing.

"She's probably freaking out right now," Gabby continued. "I stole the car. And totaled it. She's going to be so mad."

Keegan couldn't help but grin. That was something Sascha would have done, too. "Almost seventeen years ago, I met a woman named Sascha Rose. You look just like her."

A wide smile lit up Gabby's face. "Did you meet her when you dove in front of a truck to save her life in the middle of the night? In Portland, Oregon?"

Keegan fought to keep his composure. "I did."

"And then you hung out with her for a week? And it went from nice and friendly to naked time?"

Bella coughed and turned her head, trying to hide a smile.

Keegan closed his eyes for a moment, then opened them again. "Yes."

"That was my mom, who apparently lied to you about her name, so you can yell at her about that." Gabby held out her arms to the sides, as if showcasing her brilliance. "Tada! You guys made me that night. Merry Christmas, Dad. I'm home."

CHAPTER SEVEN

KEEGAN WENT DOWN to his knees, shocked. Sascha was alive? And they had a daughter?

He was too stunned to speak.

"Did I kill him?" Gabby grabbed Bella's arm. "Is he going to die? He looks like he's going to die. Does he have a bad heart?"

Bella started laughing. "No, he's just a drama queen. Keegan, stop scaring her. Get up and greet your daughter."

Keegan fought back the thousands of questions that flooded his mind, the emotions, jabbing at his gut. He struggled to hold his shit together. "I have a daughter?"

Gabby shrugged and held out her hands almost apologetically. "Mom said you wouldn't believe me. That everyone wants a piece of you." She put her hands on her hips and stood taller. "I don't want your money or anything from you. I just wanted to meet you."

Fuck. He lunged to his feet at her defensiveness. "I didn't know."

She rolled her eyes. "I know you didn't know. Obviously. My mom told me. That's why I'm here. Now you know." Her gaze met his, and her voice faded as she watched him, wariness creeping into her eyes, waiting for his response.

If he'd found out Gabby was his daughter while he was with Brody, he would have had space to react however he needed to. But with the sixteen-year-old girl staring at him, his response had to be about her. Not himself. There would be time for himself later.

And one thing he knew was that he would never, ever do the kind of damage to her that a rejection would cause. So, he shook out his shoulders and stuck out his hand. "Great to meet you, Gabby."

"You're shaking her hand?" Bella snorted. "She's your *daughter*, Keegan, not a business partner."

He shot a look at his sister, but she just grinned at him. "Hug it out, guys. This is definitely a hug moment. My first niece! This is awesome."

Gabby glanced at Bella. "You guys believe me?"

Bella nodded. "All I need to do is look at Keegan's face. He knows it's true, don't you, Keegan?"

He had no proof that Gabby was his biological daughter, but it was absolutely possible. And he did know for sure that Gabby was Sascha's kid, and that she believed that Keegan was her biological dad. He wasn't going to let Gabby down by questioning her, because he knew damn well family wasn't about blood. Family was about the heart. In Gabby's heart, he was her dad, so that was enough for him. Gabby was his daughter, end of story. "I believe you," he said, his voice rough.

Her eyes widened. "You don't want to take a paternity test or something?"

He could hear the vulnerability in her voice. He could see it in her eyes. *Hell.* He didn't know what had happened in her life or what happened to the guy Sascha had been married to at the time of her "death," but Sascha clearly had chosen him to be the guy that Gabby could believe in, that she could count on to be her dad.

He wasn't going to let either of them down. Not like how he and all his siblings had been left to fend for themselves when they'd been kids.

"No," he said. "I don't need a paternity test. I believe you."

Sudden tears filled Gabby's eyes, and she flung herself at him.

He caught her as she threw her arms around his waist and buried her face in his chest. Instinctively, he wrapped his arms around her, enfolding her against him as he met gazes with Bella.

Tears were trickling down Bella's cheeks, and her hand was over her mouth. Seeing his sister so emotional made his own throat tighten. Swearing, he shook his head once at his sister, and she grinned through her tears.

Right now, this moment, wasn't about figuring out how he was going to feel about this. It was about being the man that Gabby and Sascha needed him to be.

Sascha. *Alive.*

His gut tightened. "Gabby, we need to get you warm, and we need to call your mom. Where is she?"

Gabby pulled back, wiping the back of her hand across her cheeks. "I think she's probably following me in Jocie's car. She was tracking me on my phone until I shut it off."

He raised his brows. "You said your battery died."

She lifted her chin. "Well, it would have died if I hadn't shut it off."

He grinned. He'd spent a fair amount of time around the Stocktons, and they had enough kids to field a couple football teams, so he was used to the teenage sass, but it was still stunning how they lived by a logic that wasn't accessible to adults.

"Get in the truck before you freeze, and then we're going to turn your phone on and call her."

"Will you talk to her? She won't yell at you."

"Me?" Hell. "I haven't talked to her in almost seventeen years."

"So, it's time, then."

"I agree," said Bella. "It's the least you can do, Keegan, after failing to be a proper dad all these years."

"What?" He scowled at their giggling. "I didn't know I was a dad."

"That's a weak excuse," Bella said. "A dad should just know."

Keegan ground his jaw. "Bella—"

"You guys go ahead. I'm going to stay outside in the freezing weather and make some calls for a moment. Let the others know. You're the first of the next generation, Gabby. Everyone's going to be thrilled. Congrats, Keegan. You're the first of us to have kids, but to be honest, you didn't make it a fair contest, starting when you were eighteen."

"Life isn't fair," he said as he opened the door to his truck for Gabby. "Get used to it, sis."

"Oh, trust me, I am." She waved cheerfully, and jogged down the side of the road, leaving Keegan and Gabby alone.

He waited for the teenager to hop in, then shut the door behind her.

The moment the door was closed, he let out his breath. A daughter? He had a sixteen-year-old daughter? And Sascha was on her way to them?

Anticipation rushed through him.

He was about to see the woman he'd never forgotten.

And he was a *dad?*

CHAPTER EIGHT

SOFIA'S PHONE RANG, startling her. The freezing rain was coming down hard, and the temperature was hovering around thirty-two degrees, making the driving start to get dangerous.

She glanced at the dash, and relief rushed through her when she saw Gabby's name on the screen. She hit the answer button. "Gabby! Are you all right?"

"Hi, Mom. I totaled the car. I just need to get that out of the way first."

Sofia gripped the steering wheel. "Are you hurt?"

"No, I'm fine. I hit a patch of ice and shot off a precipice and into a canyon. But I'm fine."

Some of Sofia's tension eased. "A canyon? Really? And you're fine?"

"Yep. The car isn't, though. But it was crap anyway, so now we can get a new one."

"You won't get to drive it. You're grounded forever. Plus a day." She pulled into the parking lot of a roadside tavern so she could focus on the conversation.

"It's your fault for springing that news on me like that. I'm a fragile teenager."

Sofia started to smile, relieved to hear her daughter's sassy tone. *She really was all right.* "Where are you? Did you call a tow truck?"

"No, actually. A nice lady and her brother found me. He used a winch to pull me up out of the bottomless crevasse, but the car is still down there."

Oh, God. "Where are you now?"

"In his truck. I think he's giving me a ride. Why? Where are you?"

Sofia's hands tightened on the steering wheel. "You're in a stranger's truck?" Dear God. "Gabby. Have him drop you off at the first store you see. Get out."

"No. He's handsome and nice. I'm going with him. It'll be fine. I'm sure he won't rape and murder me."

"Gabriella!"

"Give me the phone, Gabby." A man's voice drifted over the phone. "Stop torturing her."

"Gabby! Put him on." Sofia was going to make sure he was too scared to harm a hair on her baby's head. "Let me talk to him."

"Fine. Okay. Here."

The man's voice became clearer. "Hello—"

"Who are you? I need your name, address, and license plate. I have a tracking device implanted in my daughter. I will find you and hunt you down if you hurt her—"

"Sascha."

She stopped, frozen, as the deep voice hit a chord inside her that hadn't been alive in almost seventeen years. "What did you just call me?"

"Sascha. It's Keegan Hart. She's with me."

Sofia closed her eyes and rested her forehead on the steering wheel, her heart suddenly pounding out of control. "Keegan?" Her voice was rough and raw, her throat so tight she could barely talk. He remembered her? Dear God. *He remembered her.* All these years, she'd convinced herself that she'd been nothing more than an immemorable blip in his glorious life...but she'd been *wrong*.

"Yeah." There was a long pause. "How are you, Sascha?" His voice wrapped around her, pouring into every cell in her body. "You doing all right?"

"I'm good," she whispered. "What about you?"

"Good. I just found out I'm a dad. That's always a big day in a guy's life."

Oh, *crap.* Gabby hadn't wasted any time, had she? What could Sofia say to that? Apologize? Explain what she couldn't explain? Thank him for not tossing her daughter out? "First time dad?"

Holy crap. Had she really just said that? Made a freaking *joke*? There were probably a billion meaningful, emotional, heart-felt things she could have said, that she *should* have said, but instead, she made a *joke*?

There was another long pause as he apparently processed her blithe comment. "Yep," he finally said. "I'm guessing she's getting the car keys taken away from her? I want to be on the same page. No divide and conquer."

"Hey!" Gabby protested.

"No keys," Sofia agreed. "Right."

"Got it. Any other rules?"

"She's not allowed to go after you and tell you that you're her biological father." Yeah, how was she going to explain that rule? That she'd hidden his daughter from him all these years?

"Great. I'll add that to the list. I assume she's a good kid who always follows the rules?"

"I am a good kid," Gabby protested. "This called for extreme measures."

"She's a wonderful kid," Sofia said softly. "Please keep her safe."

"Of course. I'm good at protecting people." He paused. "Are you on your way here? Gabby said you were."

She let out her breath. She could tell him to send Gabby home. She'd never have to see him. Pop her daughter on his private jet and ship her back to Seattle. Never face what had happened, and what might have been. Never risk getting in the papers by hanging around a celebrity who the press loved to write about. Slink back to her store and keep living the same, safe little life she'd lived for years.

And miss out on the chance to see the man she'd never forgotten about.

"Sascha? Are you still there? Did we lose you?"

She let out her breath. "I'm on my way there," she said. *Holy cow! She was going!* "GPS says I'm about two hours away, but the roads are getting slick. It'll probably take me longer."

"Do you have chains for your car?"

She smiled at his question. Still the same Keegan who wanted to keep her safe. That was how they'd met, and he was still the same guy. "No, but it's not that bad. I'll be okay."

"Tell me where you are."

"Were you this bossy when I knew you before?"

"I just pulled Gabby out of a ditch because of the ice, and I'd rather not do the same to you. Where are you?"

She sighed. That was incredibly sweet, which was super annoying. "Fine. I'm in the parking lot of a restaurant called Black Bear Tavern."

"I know where that is. Do you have chains for your tires?"

"No—"

"Stay there. The roads are too icy. We'll be there in a couple hours."

"A couple hours? No, I'm coming to you—"

"Sascha." His voice was low and rough, sending chills down her spine. "You have a sixteen-year-old kid who needs her mom not to die on a mountain."

She sighed. "You're so annoying."

She could almost feel his grin at her capitulation. "The food's pretty good. Have some lunch. We'll see you soon."

"Fine." She hated that it felt good to have him save Gabby and be worried about her welfare. She hated that it showed her that he was the same protector that she'd fallen so hard for the first time. "Drive carefully. That's my baby you have there."

"Mine too, apparently."

She closed her eyes. *Crap.*

"Mom?"

Her heart turned over at the sound of her daughter's voice. "Yes?"

"I love you."

Her heart tightened. "I love you, too—"

"We'll see you soon! You have two hours to come up with a reason to explain to Keegan why you never told him about me. Can't wait to hear the reason, too! Bye!"

Oh for heaven's sake. "Gabby—"

But Gabby had already hung up.

Holy crap.

Sofia leaned back in the seat and clasped her hands on her head, her mind whirling over the phone call. Keegan still called her Sascha. He knew nothing about her, or what had happened. And yet he'd accepted without question that Gabby was his daughter.

Sudden tears filled her eyes. "Thank you, Keegan," she whispered. "Thank you for not breaking my baby's heart."

How much did he remember about their time together? About how it had ended?

Based on his response to Gabby, she was guessing he remembered everything.

How was she going to explain that last night? And explain the fact that she'd hidden his daughter from him all this time?

For the last sixteen years, he'd been a shadow in her heart. Seven days of magic with a stranger. A romance that had never had the chance to run its course.

And now she was on an icy mountain in the Cascade mountains, waiting for him to show up, with a daughter who was going to bind them together.

Lock them together.

Trap them together.

How much could those days have meant? How much foundation did that give them to handle today?

What had they meant to him?

And what would it mean in two hours, when he walked into that tavern?

CHAPTER NINE

KEEGAN PAUSED in the parking lot of the Black Bear Tavern, waiting for Bella and Gabby to get out of the truck. The two were already pals, and Bella's welcome of Gabby had been instant and genuine. Being one of two girls in a family with seven boys, Bella had always wanted more women.

And now she had one.

But...what the hell?

He took a breath, taking the first moment of privacy to breathe.

He had a daughter.

Sascha was alive.

Since he'd picked up Gabby, he'd been entirely focused on her. Making her feel comfortable. Trying to ease the tension. Hiding his shock at what had happened. He didn't have time to process, to connect with her, and he wouldn't have time before he had to face Sascha...who was inside that building.

He scanned the old log cabin-style tavern. The parking lot was fairly empty, because it was that time of the afternoon between lunch and dinner. *Sascha was in there.*

Holy crap.

The door slammed, and Gabby and Bella got out. Gabby was holding Millie in her arms. "She didn't want to be left alone. She wants her papa."

He held out his arms, and Millie tumbled out of Gabby's arms into his. He put her in his jacket so that only her head was poking out, then frowned when he saw Bella and Gabby gazing at him. "What?"

"That's literally so cute you put a puppy in your jacket," Bella said. "You're like this big, bubbling pile of mush, and I had no idea."

"I'm not mush." He shifted restlessly. "You think you should go in first, Gabby? Work things out with your mom? I can wait out here. Or you want me to go in first?" He prided himself on always having his shit together, but suddenly, he felt like an awkward teenager again. What if Sascha banned him from seeing Gabby ever? What would happen when he saw her again? What if sixteen years of memories had made her into something she wasn't?

He realized Bella and Gabby were staring at him. "What?"

Bella nudged Gabby. "He's freaking out about seeing your mom again."

Gabby frowned. "Really? Why?"

"He's been obsessed with her this whole time. My brother's been looking for since she left, but he never found her."

Gabby's face grew wary. "You've been looking for her?"

"I'm not a stalker. I wasn't looking. Brody was." He frowned at the sudden tension in Gabby's body. She'd been so relaxed since she'd been there, that the quick shift was noticeable. "What's wrong?"

Gabby paced restlessly away from them. "You guys have to promise you won't tell anyone about us. That you know who we are. That you found out. You can't tell the press. Promise not to tell the press?"

Bella and Keegan exchanged glances again, and the pieces

began to come together in Keegan's mind. Sascha had faked her death with her daughter. Whether the accident was real and she decided afterwards to take advantage or whether the accident was a fake didn't matter. What mattered was that Sascha had gone deep underground for sixteen years, and her daughter had broken cover to come find him. *Shit.*

"Who's after you?" he asked softly. "Who are you guys hiding from?" Her ex-husband was his first guess.

Gabby stared at him, her lips pressed together.

Shit.

"We'll make sure you and your mom are safe," Keegan said. "Promise."

"What about the press? Promise you won't let them find out."

He glanced at Bella again. "I don't control the press, Gabby, but they won't hear it from us."

She still looked worried, and he met Bella's gaze. He knew his sister had picked up on all the same signals he had. Noticing threats and being aware when a kid was in danger was habit to them, given their history. Always hitting too close to home.

Bella inclined her chin once, then turned to Gabby. "Don't worry, Gabby. Now that Brody married Tatum, they are the big news. No one is paying attention to us out here. This is our neck of the woods. We're not interesting here."

Gabby nodded, then glanced at Keegan.

"We'll keep you safe, Gabby," he said softly. "It's what we do."

She raised her brows. "You're tech-geeks turned billionaires."

"We're street kids who never forgot how to protect our own." He kept his voice low and rough, letting her see the truth about who he was, who Bella was, and who they all were.

53

Her eyes widened, and then a grin lit up her face. "Cool."

SOFIA WRAPPED her hands around the mug of hot chocolate, her knee bouncing restlessly. Christmas music enveloped her as she sat under strands of twinkling white lights. A Christmas tree sat in the corner, with lots of unwrapped presents beneath it for a local women's shelter. The tavern was charming and rustic, and the servers knew most of the patrons.

It felt like a home. Her waitress was named Becca, and she'd been so friendly and warm that Sofia had started to relax. She'd gotten a window seat, but she didn't look out. What was the point? Watch every truck?

"Mom!"

Sofia looked up, and relief rushed through her when she saw her daughter running toward her across the tavern. She jumped up and had barely made it to her feet before Gabby reached her and flung herself into her arms. "I'm so sorry I took the car, Mom. I'm sorry if I put us in danger."

All her tension dissolved, and she hugged Gabby tightly, tears rimming her eyes. "I'm just glad you're okay, baby. I was so worried."

Gabby pulled back, her eyes wide. "I just had to go. I had to know. And he's wonderful. And his sister Bella is amazing. They welcomed me, Mom. They didn't even question me at all. Who's like that? He doesn't want proof. He just said, okay."

Sofia's heart tightened. The papers always made the Harts sound like good people, but their welcoming Gabby so whole-heartedly was a gift Sofia would never forget. "I'm glad."

"Me, too." Gabby's face was troubled. "I told them not to tell the press about me. About us."

Oh, *God*. "What else did you tell them?"

"Nothing, I swear. Just not to tell anyone."

Movement behind Gabby caught Sofia's attention. She tensed and looked behind her daughter, but it wasn't Keegan. It was a woman, maybe around thirty. She was in jeans, a cowboy hat, and winter boots. "Hi," she said, "I'm Bella. I don't know if you remember me, but we met back then."

Sofia swallowed. "I remember meeting you, but I wouldn't have recognized you."

"I was a homeless waif back then. Not much to recognize today." Warmth filled Bella's eyes. "It's great to see you again. You have a wonderful daughter."

Sofia smiled as Gabby pulled away. "I know. She's my whole heart—" At that moment, Keegan walked into the tavern.

Her breath caught when she saw him. He was taller than she remembered, broader. He was wearing a cowboy hat, jeans, and a dark blue shirt open at the neck. He was pure muscle and man, and every bit of her body seemed to come alive at the sight of him. And there was a tiny, scraggly dog peeking out from the front of his jacket. "Holy crap," she whispered.

"Right? He's magnetic." Bella tugged on Gabby's arm. "Let's hit the bathroom while the grownups are distracted."

Gabby grinned. "Bye, Mom! Love you!"

"But—"

"It might take us a while. You know how long it takes girls to go to the bathroom," Bella said. "Great to see you again, Sascha!" The two made a break for the bathroom, ignoring Sofia's attempts to stop them.

She could tell Gabby was safe and happy with Bella... family that Gabby deserved to know.

But she didn't want to be alone with Keegan. Maybe she should run for the bathroom, too...

But her feet seemed stuck to the floor.

Her heart pounding, she watched Keegan. When his gaze met hers, he stiffened, and came to a complete stop, his hand moving to rest on the dog's head, as if he was grounding himself through the shaggy little canine, which was just too adorable for her to even deal with.

For what felt like an eternity, neither of them moved. They just stared at each other across the dimly lit tavern.

Dear God. He was *breathtaking*. Not in a sculpted model kind of way. In that rough, untamed, protective way that had captivated her so long ago.

Attraction? Still there. *Crap*.

He began to walk toward her, and her heart seemed to beat faster with each step he took, until it seemed to blend into one frantic vibration of tension, all tangled up with desire, attraction, and embarrassment.

How could she possibly explain everything that had happened?

He came to a stop a few feet away, his blue eyes fixed on hers. "Sascha," he said, his voice rough and compelling as it brushed over her skin.

Oh God. His voice was amazing. She swallowed. "Keegan," she whispered. "You look great."

His gaze was veiled as it settled on her face. "You look complicated," he said.

She started laughing as the tension eased from her. Same Keegan. "Oh, you have no idea."

"Are you going to tell me?"

And just like that, the tension was back.

CHAPTER TEN

KEEGAN FELT like every cell in his body was on fire as he stood there in that tavern, only an arm's length from the woman he'd never forgotten.

Sascha was here.

It was taking all his willpower not to close the distance between them, sweep her up in his arms, and kiss her until the sixteen years of silence vanished.

Her voice, when she'd said his name, had felt like coming home. No one said his name the way she did. A little rough, a little throaty, with the kind of warmth that made a man feel like he'd finally found the place he belonged.

For a kid who'd been homeless since the age of twelve, home was a big freaking deal.

Sascha's breath was shallow as she gazed up at him, the turquoise frames of her glasses not hiding those deep brown eyes that used to swallow him up.

Fuck. He was in trouble, wasn't he?

"I don't even know where to start," she said. "It's a lot."

"I gathered." He had so much to say. So much he wanted

to know. But the words stuck in his throat. All he wanted was to be in the present with her. To breathe this moment in.

"I'm going to check on Gabby," she blurted out. She tried to bolt past him, but her shoulder brushed against his chest. She sucked in her breath at the same moment he did, and they locked gazes as he closed his hand gently around her wrist drawing her to a stop, while he kept his other hand on Millie, just to make sure she was safe.

"Almost seventeen years," he said softly. "How does it still feel like this to be around you?"

Sascha shook her head. "I don't know. It shouldn't. It was a week. There shouldn't be anything here."

Ahh...she felt it, too.

She looked up at him, her face so close to his. All he'd have to do would be to lean in, and her lips would be under his.

Her eyes widened. "No, don't."

He closed his eyes for a moment to pull his shit together. "I would never do anything without your permission."

"But you wanted to kiss me." It wasn't a question.

"I did."

"Why?"

He smiled. "Because you're still you. Irresistible to me."

"No." She took a step back, toward the table. "Why aren't you mad?" she asked. "About Gabby? About that night? How can you look at me like you want to kiss me, instead of shout at me?"

She had her hands on her hips and her chin up. Defensive posture. Ready to be attacked.

He shrugged and moved past her to sit down at her table, refusing to escalate.

Life under the bridge had taught all of the Harts that people did some serious shit when pushed to the edge. He'd done stuff. His siblings had as well. Lots of crap had happened at the hands of the Harts during desperate moments. "Seems pretty asinine to be mad before I have facts. You might have great reasons for all of it." He nodded at the table, indicating that she might take a seat. "Or you might just be a cold-hearted, evil sociopath."

She blinked. "I'm not a sociopath."

"Didn't figure you were, but I thought I'd give you an out. You sitting down?" He unzipped his jacket a bit and cradled Millie against his chest. She licked his chin, a sweet gesture that eased some of his tension.

"Yeah." Sofia eased into the opposite bench of the booth. "What's your dog's name?"

"Millie. I found her behind a dumpster a couple days ago. She was hungry and homeless, so..." he shrugged.

A smile flickered at the corners of Sofia's mouth. "Of course you had to save her. And bring her with you."

He nodded. "I couldn't let her be alone anymore."

"No. You couldn't." She took a breath. "Keegan?"

Damn, she smelled good. "What?"

"I just want you to know that I will be grateful until the day I die for how you reacted when Gabby showed up today. You are a stunning human being. Thank you for not pushing her away."

His heart seemed to twist in his chest. Her love for Gabby was pouring out of her like sunshine. Gabby was a lucky kid to have Sascha as her mom. The teenager would never have to doubt if she were loved...by her mom at least. "Is she really my kid, Sascha? Don't get me wrong, I'll claim her either way. But is she mine?"

Sascha searched his face. "You mean that, don't you? You literally will claim her even if I said she wasn't your biological daughter?"

"Yeah. She believes I'm her dad. I'm not going to let her down. If she's not my biological daughter, I figure you had a reason to tell her I was, so I'm not going to abandon her just because she doesn't carry the same DNA as I do. The Harts don't give a shit about blood ties when it comes to family, as you know."

She smiled. "I do know that."

He rubbed his fingers over Millie's scruffy head. "Plus, logistically, she could be mine, so I'm not stepping away from that responsibility."

Sascha's eyes glistened. "I was wrong not to tell you," she whispered. "I'm sorry. God, I'm so sorry, Keegan. I didn't know what to do, and—"

Her grief was so palpable he felt it wrap around him. He gave up resisting. He got up, went around to her side of the table, sat down beside her, and pulled her into his arms. Not to kiss her. To hold her.

She stiffened, and he thought she was going to pull back.

Then suddenly, her body softened, her arms went around his waist, and she sagged into him, pressing her face into his chest, Millie tucked happily between them.

He closed his eyes, breathing in the feel of Sascha's body against his. Their time together had been so fleeting. It had happened so long ago. And yet, the feel of her body against his was so familiar, so *right*.

There was so much to unpack between them. So much he needed to know. Things that could very well unravel this bond they still had, a bond that was built on fragile filaments of fleeting moments and stolen freedoms so long ago. Gossamer threads held them together, glistening in the icy pre-Christmas sparkle.

Threads that might break at any moment.

But in this moment, they were still, surprisingly, intact.

So, he sat there, holding her, refusing to move, breathing in the moment for as long as they had it.

It was more than he'd had in almost seventeen years, so he'd take it.

CHAPTER ELEVEN

Keegan smelled delicious.

He was muscled.

He was strong.

And his arms felt familiar, safe, and, if Sofia were honest with herself, *thrilling.* Like how she used to feel with him. And the little puppy in his jacket made her remember how soft his heart had been back then, so gentle, despite all he'd been through.

"Damn you." She pulled back. "You feel ridiculously good. Aren't you supposed to be old and decrepit now?"

Keegan grinned. "I'm unequivocally opposed to becoming old and decrepit." He cocked an eyebrow. "You look fantastic, by the way."

A warm, fuzzy feeling settled inside her, and she smiled. "Thank you. You look like you're stripping me naked with your eyes."

He had the grace not to look remotely embarrassed. "It's nothing inappropriate. Just trying to figure out if you're a walking zombie. You know. Since you've been dead for fifteen years."

She wrinkled her nose. "You thought I was dead?"

"As of a couple days ago, yeah." He shrugged. "But only for a short time, so I'm over it." His eyes were turbulent and dark, making her pretty sure he wasn't over any of it at all. He gestured toward the bathroom. "Gabby will be back any moment, so let's say what we need to say before she gets back."

"Right. I'm sure we can get through all this in a minute or two."

Amusement flashed in his eyes. "Nothing much to talk about, really," he agreed, with a tone that said he didn't agree at all. "Just curious really about what brand of vanilla extract you use. I'm always interested to hear what folks are using these days."

"Local brand. Very nice." Oh, God. This was excruciating. She needed to focus and get through the tough part. She took a breath, trying to hold down her attraction to him. She hadn't dated or been with anyone for years. She'd thought that she was over that. But being around Keegan had lit something up inside her...just like before. "Look, we don't want anything from you—"

"Who are you hiding from?"

She stared at him, her mouth dropping open. "What?"

"You faked your death. Gabby is clearly worried that someone will find you." His arm tightened along the back of the cushion, encircling her. "Who are you hiding from?"

She stared at him. "You don't want to know about what happened that last night we were together? Why I left? Why I didn't tell you that you have a daughter?"

His eyes were turbulent. "Oh, I want to know all of that, but none of that matters if you two wind up dead just because Gabby decided to track me down. That would be a pretty crappy Christmas for all involved, and I like Christmas, so I kinda want to keep it on the no-death side this year. So, priorities. What's the threat?"

His need to protect her was exactly the same as it had been when they'd met. Instant. Instinctive. And ridiculously attractive. She shook her head at him and pushed at his immoveable shoulder. "No. You don't get to go all heroic on us. I don't need that."

He raised his brows. "Clearly, you don't need it. You've been fine for the last sixteen years, both of you alive and well. However, I need it. It's in my DNA to protect. That's my kid in the bathroom, right? Because regardless of how you feel about me, I have a vested interest in keeping my own daughter safe, even if I just met her."

Fear trickled down Sofia's spine, and suddenly, she felt trapped. "You don't get to take over our life, Keegan. That's not what this is about. She wanted to meet you, and that's it. When she gets out of the bathroom, we're going home."

His eyes darkened. "Sascha," he said softly. "It's not that easy between us. You know it's not—"

"Sofia. My name is Sofia. I lied to you when I told you it was Sascha. I didn't want those seven days to become more, for you to be able to find me." She was pushing him away. She could feel it. Panic was closing in, and she wanted space, freedom, to run.

He said nothing, but his eyes were thoughtful as he studied her, gently scratching Millie's head, still taking care of the puppy regardless of the tension between them, because he was like that. Always the protector. Always with the kindness.

He didn't rise to her bait. Of course he didn't. He was more chill than that. She'd never been able to get a rise from him, not even that terrible night.

He, however, could work her up with zero effort whatsoever. Like now. She became aware that she had scooted back into the corner of the booth, as far away from him as she could get, her hands up defensively, as if she had to protect herself physically.

She dropped her hand and sat taller, but not before Keegan saw her instinctive response.

"Would you like me to call you Sofia?" he asked, his voice still low and even. Did nothing rattle him? "Or would you prefer I call you Sascha?"

"My name is Sofia."

"That's not what I asked."

Dammit. How could he read her that well? She did want him to call her Sascha. It made her feel like a teenager again, caught up in an illicit love affair. It reminded her of a time when it was safe to fall in love with a teenage rogue who swept her heart up into his kind hands and captured her heart with his. "Call me Sofia."

He nodded slowly. "You're sure?"

"Stop it. Just stop it." Her heart was pounding now, and she could feel every cell in her body screaming at her to run. She wasn't in danger, but old instincts were running rampant with her mind right now. "He was handsome, like you," she blurted out. "He swept me off my feet. I couldn't think. I didn't even know what had happened before I was married to him. I had no defenses against him, just like I have no defenses against you. It feels the same with you. I know it's not, but it feels like it is." She held up her hand, showing how it was trembling. "I'm literally shaking."

She hadn't meant to tell him, but she'd survived the last decade and a half because she'd learned to process her emotions instead of keeping them bottled up until they exploded. Like before, Keegan had already broken down her walls, somehow transcending the distance she was trying to keep between them.

Keegan's face softened, and he took her hand, curling his

larger one around hers and brushing his lips over it. The warmth and strength in his made tears threaten. He was like a giant teddy bear with a black belt in karate. Pretty much a perfect combination. "You're safe with me," he said.

Sofia raised her chin. "He said the same thing. That's how he got me. I was eighteen, in the hospital alone, about to give birth. I had nothing. He told me I was safe. And I needed that. I needed someone to make me safe. Staying with someone because they will make you safe isn't the right reason. It disempowers. It traps. I don't want you to keep me safe. I don't." But she couldn't make herself pull away from Keegan's touch. "I need to be in charge of my own safety."

His touch felt so good. Safe, but also more than safe. His touch felt like life, like a free spirit, like the liberation of her heart.

"Sascha—"

"When Gabby gets back, I'm going to take her home," she said. "I'm guessing she'll want to keep in touch, so that's fine, if you want to do that. It would crush her if I didn't let her build a relationship with you, if you want to. But not with me. You and I aren't keeping in touch." She met his gaze. "I've been independent for years now, Keegan. I won't trade that in for a trap."

A muscle in his cheek ticked in irritation, surprising her. He never let on with his emotions. Even as she said it, she knew she didn't want to leave with Gabby. She wanted to sit there on that bench with Keegan forever, basking in that pull she felt toward him.

But she would leave. Just like before—

"Mom!" Gabby came bounding over to the table, and Sofia instantly pulled her hand away from Keegan's, and dragged her gaze off his. "Bella said we can go with them to finish this delivery route, and then go back to their ranch.

They have a family pre-Christmas get-together tomorrow night, and she wants me to come meet everyone!"

Oh, God. "Gabby—"

"Look!" Gabby grabbed Bella's phone and held it out to her. "*Look!*"

Glancing at Bella's beaming face and Keegan's frowning one, Sofia took the phone. It was open to a group text called "Hart Family."

There was a text from Colin Hart that said, *Can't wait to meet Gabby.*

And a text from Dylan Hart that said, *I'm out of town, but I'll change my plans to be back for the party. Gotta make up for lost time with her.*

And a text from Brody Hart. *Fuck, Bella. Alive? They're both alive? Damn straight I want to meet them. Keegan must be losing his shit to have Sascha back and to have a kid. Tatum and I will both be there tomorrow. Tell Gabby she's one of us and always will be. She's got a second family now.*

Tears filled Sofia's eyes and she put the phone down on the table. "How can you guys be like that? I don't understand."

"Because that's who we are," Bella said, sitting down across from Sofia. "Family is literally all we have. The money is secondary. Family is what matters, both the kind you create and the kind you're born into." She smiled at Gabby. "Can't wait to get to know you better, Gabby. We need more girl power in this family."

Sofia sat back in her seat, watching her daughter, her precious one-and-only, pluck Millie from Keegan's arms, and then cuddle the dog while she chatted animatedly with Bella. Gabby was so thrilled to be a part of the Harts, to have this instant huge family who all loved her.

Suddenly, Sofia felt woefully inadequate. She'd always

worked so hard to be enough for Gabby, to give her the security and support she needed. But as she watched Gabby come to life with Keegan, Bella, and Millie, she knew she hadn't done enough, been enough.

She wanted nothing more than to grab her kid, take her home, and pretend none of this had ever happened.

But Pandora's Box had been opened, as she'd known it would.

There was no way to close it without destroying her daughter, and probably Sofia's relationship with her.

Gabby's smile faded at Sofia's silence. "Mom? We can go, can't we?"

"Look," Keegan said. "Your car isn't safe to drive right now anyway. We'll finish the deliveries today, and then head back. You guys meet everyone, then crash at my place. I'll send someone to get your car, we'll get you some tire chains, and then you can head back."

She sighed. "Keegan—"

"Sascha." He lowered his voice, just for her, but she was aware of Bella and Gabby leaning in.

She shifted restlessly. "What?"

"I will not trap you or Gabby. I swear it."

She said nothing.

"Tell the gremlin in your head that's freaking out to take a two-minute break so you can think clearly."

She raised her brows. "That works?"

"Yeah, it does." He grinned, showcasing two adorable dimples. "Try it."

Sofia took a deep breath, and asked the gremlin in her head to take a two-minute break from freaking out. To her surprise, she felt the panic ease off slightly, and she could suddenly breathe again. Suddenly, she felt the tension ease from her body.

Keegan wasn't like her ex. He never would be like her ex. And deep in her heart, she'd known that. If she hadn't been absolutely certain he was a good man, she never would have told Gabby his name, regardless of the promise she'd made to her daughter.

Keegan *was* Gabby's biological dad, and if both he and Gabby wanted to make it real, well, her daughter deserved it. It was scary as hell for Sofia, but what could she do? All that mattered was her daughter's well-being, and honestly, it would be a tremendous relief to know that if anything ever happened to her, Gabby would never have to be alone.

"Mom? Please? I want to go with them." Gabby paused. "I want *us* to go with them."

As Gabby stared at her hopefully, Sofia suddenly knew that they had to go. Keegan was an unresolved part of both their pasts, and neither of them would be whole until it was faced. She had to go, not just for Gabby, but for herself...as difficult as it would be. Sofia managed a smile. "Well, I'm certainly not about to let you ride off into the sunset with some strange man and his sidekick all by yourself."

"Yay!" Gabby squealed with delight. "You're the best, Mom!"

"Perfect!" Bella looked thrilled as well. "I knew we were meant to go on this road trip. We were supposed to find each other."

While Gabby started to grill Bella about their next stop, Sofia looked over at Keegan. He was watching her thoughtfully, looking so insanely tempting that she knew she should have said no...and equally glad she hadn't.

"Just one more thing," Bella said.

Sofia looked over at her. "What's that?"

"It's an overnight trip."

Sofia blinked. "Overnight?"

Bella winked. "Yep. A sleepover. We rented rooms at a nice hotel in the mountains, so I'm sure there are plenty of rooms for all."

Oh, God. Sleeping in the same building as Keegan? She'd never survive it.

CHAPTER TWELVE

THIRTY MINUTES INTO THEIR DRIVE, Sofia knew she was in trouble. As far as awkward moments went, she was pretty sure she'd found the winner.

Not just an awkward moment. It was a painful, interminable arduous awkwardness...and they'd only been in the car for a half hour.

How was she going to get through the next twenty-four hours?

She'd considered bolting about a thousand times, but every time, she would watch Gabby leaning forward over the seat, to chat excitedly with Keegan and Bella.

The bond was growing fast between the three of them, which was both great and terrifying.

Was she going to lose her kid to this exciting, rich, big, celebrity family?

Bella and Keegan had tried to get Sofia to sit in the front seat, but she had declined. This was about Gabby, not her. Well, maybe it was also about her facing Keegan and unraveling what had been so tangled up for so long, but that conversation wasn't going to happen until they were alone... which wasn't when the four of them were sharing his truck.

Keegan hadn't looked happy when Sofia had refused the front seat, but he'd given her that thoughtful, assessing look again, and then conceded.

She'd been happy at first to be able to retreat, but now, as she sat there in the corner of the back seat, she felt like she didn't fit. The other three tried to engage her in conversation, but she just felt too uncomfortable.

Maybe it would have been better if she and Keegan had had time to really talk. Right now, there was so much unsaid that it made the air thick with emotion. At least for her.

Her phone dinged, and she looked down to see a text from Jocie. *You're staying with him tonight? Seriously? Baby #2?*

Sofia felt her cheeks heat up. *Don't even. It's incredibly awkward. We haven't even had a chance to speak more than a minute because Bella and Gabby are here.*

You need to ditch them, then.

Sofia sighed. *She's my kid. He's her dad. I'm not going to ditch her so I can be alone with him.*

Babe, you can't be a good mom if you don't take care of yourself. You have to get him alone. Hash it out. Get naked.

Sofia paused for a moment as Keegan, Bella, and Gabby burst out laughing. Her heart turned over at the sound of pure joy and adulation in her daughter's voice, and the way she gazed at Keegan as if he were her hero. She looked down at her phone again. *I'm scared, Jocie. I'm scared I'm going to lose her to these people and this life.*

F*ck that. You're one of a kind, and Gabby knows it. You guys have a bond that will never break. You're good. She's good. Enjoy the ride. And make sure you're back by Monday night when we have the Christmas party. You can't miss that.

The Christmas party. She'd forgotten about that. *Okay. Thanks.*

Get him alone. You guys have to talk, especially if he and Gabby continue to build a relationship. Even if you don't get naked, you have to get comfortable with him.

I know. I know. You're right. I'll find a way. She looked up suddenly and saw Keegan watching her in the rearview mirror. His gaze was intense and thoughtful, rich with unspoken words. Her belly turned over as she realized that Keegan was as aware of her as she was of him.

He'd seemed to be entirely focused on Gabby, but he was still waiting for that moment with her.

Excitement and nervousness warred in her, and she averted her gaze, too agitated to smile at him. She knew, though, that he was going to make sure they had time to talk tonight.

Alone.

And then all the truth would have to come out.

～

KEEGAN PULLED his gaze off Sascha and back to the road, frowning as he carefully navigated the icy roads with his precious cargo.

The biggest thing about Sascha had been her free spirit and her inner light...but that light was dim right now. She was holding herself small in the back of his truck, and he wasn't okay with that.

He couldn't ask any personal questions right now, not with Gabby and Bella there, but he could do what they'd done seventeen years ago, and have fun with what they had.

He tightened his grip on the steering wheel in resolve as he turned into a dirt parking lot for a log-cabin general store called Alice's. "First stop," he said. Alice's. Damn. He remembered this place. It had been a long time. "Alice was the first person who bought anything from me. I used to bring her stuff for free, and she's the one who insisted on paying me."

He opened his truck just as the front door of the store opened. An older woman with gray hair, hiking boots and jeans came out on the porch. A tall woman who still looked strong, she put her hands on her hips. "Well, if it isn't Keegan Hart. Too big for your britches to come and see us?"

He grinned and jogged up the steps to wrap the older lady up in a hug. "Never too big for you, Alice."

She hugged him back, her blue eyes glistening as she put her hands on his cheeks. "I've been watching you, my boy. I'm so proud of what you've done with your bakery. So proud. You started here, remember?"

"I do." He was suddenly so glad he'd come. Bella had been right. He'd needed to get back out on the road, and connect with the people and the reason he'd fallen in love with baking in the first place. Baking was about keeping the memory of his mom alive, doing justice to the home she'd created, to the love she'd shown. Not some corporate numbers crap. "Sorry I haven't been back. I got lost," he said quietly.

Alice smiled. "Haven't you heard? Not all who wander are lost." She gestured at the truck. "Who did you bring with you?"

He looked back at the truck. Suddenly, he was overwhelmed with emotion as his gaze landed on the three females walking toward him. His sister. His *daughter*. And Sascha.

He cleared his throat, trying to stay focused. "My sister, Bella. Bella, this is Alice. She was my first supporter."

"I'm so happy to meet you!" Bella hugged Alice.

Alice gave Bella some love, then her gaze went to Gabby and Sascha. "You have a daughter?"

He raised his brows, startled by her observation. "What?

"She has your eyes!" Alice held out her hands to Gabby. "Tell me your name, and why I never met you before."

"My name's Gabriella," Gabby said. "Keegan and I just found out about each other, so it's all new."

Oh, *crap*. Teenagers.

Sascha grimaced, and Alice immediately raised her brows at Sascha. "She looks just like you. What's your name? You're Mom, right?"

Sascha nodded. "My name's Sofia—"

"You've been holding this massive secret all this time, Sofia? You didn't tell either one of them about the other? Gabriella is what, fifteen? Sixteen? And you hid who her dad was this entire time?"

Sascha's cheeks turned pink, and Keegan swore under his breath. "It's fine," he said quickly. "We're working it out. Not a big deal."

"It is a big deal," Alice said. "You lied to them both?" she asked Sascha.

"Alice," Keegan warned, but Sascha pulled her shoulders back.

"Yes," she said, her voice strong and defensive. "Gabby's sixteen, and yes, I didn't tell either of them. It's complicated—"

"Of course it is." Alice said. "I had one of those."

Sascha blinked. "One of what?"

"A secret baby daddy. Sometimes you have to do that." Alice gave Sascha a look of such understanding. "It's a hell of a burden to carry."

Sascha's eyes glistened with sudden tears, but she shrugged, clearly trying to play it off, but not before Keegan saw her reaction.

Shit.

They all stared at the older lady in surprise. "Really?" Sascha finally asked.

"Yep. Give yourself a break, and the two of you—" She leveled a hard look at Keegan and Gabby. "You both give her a break, too. Got it?"

"Got it." Keegan grinned, and Gabby nodded.

"All right, then, bring me my food." Alice held the door open. "I assume you're bringing my Christmas goodies? If so, bring 'em in, kiddos! We're almost out!" She switched topics as if she had not just unlocked a fully loaded conversation. "Sofia, come with me inside."

Keegan started to go with Alice and Sascha, but the older lady held up her hand. "Give us a sec, Cowboy. Gotta do some girl talk. Go."

Keegan frowned, but he caught Sofia's eye, silently asking her if she wanted him to intervene. She met his gaze, then shook her head. "It's fine."

"All right, then." He fished Millie out of his coat and handed her to Sascha, who tucked her against her chest, holding the tiny furball. "Can you hold onto her while I bring stuff in?"

Alice's eyes widened. "You got a dog?"

"She was homeless," he said simply.

"Of course." Alice smiled. "All right. You know where the goodies go. Come on, Sofia."

CHAPTER THIRTEEN

Sofia did not want to do the secret-baby-bonding thing with Alice.

She didn't want to rehash the past.

She didn't want a stranger to give her permission to hold the secret she'd already held.

But she was happy to have Millie tucked against her chest, so she decided to focus on that, and just get the discussion out of the way with Alice. She could tell the older woman wasn't going to let up until she'd gotten out whatever she wanted to say, so Sofia steeled herself to just get through it, hoping at least that judgment and lectures would be minimal.

But the moment Sofia stepped into the store, she forgot about her anti-social mood. "This shop is adorable." It was a rustic general store, and it was filled with Christmas cheer. A decorated tree in the corner, Christmas lights strung around the walls, a life-sized stuffed reindeer in the corner. It actually reminded her a lot of her bookstore, and she felt instantly at home. "I love it!"

"Thank you, my dear. It's been a labor of love for several

generations. My sister owns a similar store in Birch Crossing, Maine, and she loves it, too. When you love your work, you never work, right?"

"That's so true," Sofia agreed. "I run a romance bookstore. I have the best customers."

"Customers make all the difference," Alice said brightly. "Are you having a Christmas party for them?"

"I am, actually. Monday evening. I'm excited. It's always fun."

"I bet it is." Alice gestured her through the store, past tables with red checkered tablecloths, where a few Hart bakery items were displayed. "To the back, my dear." She hustled Sofia through double doors and into a storage room, which was full of boxes. The minute the door closed behind her, she spun toward Sofia. "Girl talk."

"Okay." Sofia hugged the puppy against her chest.

"That was an incredibly unenthusiastic response." Alice raised her brows. "Not interested in what I have to say?"

Crap. She didn't want to be rude. "No. I just—"

"You don't need permission to do what you did, and you don't want me to offer it. I get it. I was like you." Alice sat down on a stack of newspapers. "Damn straight you don't need permission. I wasn't going to offer it. Maybe some congrats on making a tough call, but you probably don't want that either."

Sofia relaxed a little. "Then what's our secret chat for?"

"I can do the math. I know you knew Keegan Hart before he was gracing the covers of *People* magazine."

Sofia had no idea where this was going. "Yes."

"Well, then, there's something I need to say." Alice met her gaze. "That man out in my store might be rich, he might be a celebrity, and he might have a string of women who want a piece of him, but he's one of the most decent human beings I've ever met."

Sofia let out a breath. "I know."

"Do you?" Alice leaned forward. "Now that your secret's out, you don't need to be afraid of him. However you want this to shake out, he'll respect it and make it happen. So, quit looking so damned scared! Now that you don't need to fight so hard to hide the truth, you can take a deep breath, relax, maybe giggle a little with this freaking handsome as hell escort, and let the Christmas spirit seep into your bones."

Sofia grinned, finally relaxing. "That wasn't the speech I thought I was going to get."

"Probably not, but it was the one you needed." Alice stood up. "My bones have seen a lot of decades. They're wise and smart and they know that each moment is a gift. Every damn one. So drop those shields and just let this unfold however it was meant to. Because you deserve to have a little bit of fun, my dear. Take it."

Sofia felt the rest of the tension easing from her body, making her aware of how tightly she'd been holding herself. She smiled. "Thank you. I did need that speech."

"I told you I was wise." Alice headed toward the door, then paused. "One more thing."

"What's that?"

"If you open your heart and discover that it wants Keegan to fill it up, trust your instincts. He's a good man, and he looks at you with the expression that I've been hoping to see on his face since the day I met him ten years ago and realized what a good person he was."

Sudden hope hammered in Sofia's chest. "What expression is that?"

"Like he never stopped loving you."

"He doesn't—"

"I know him, and I know what I see. And you look at him the same way."

Sofia's mouth dropped open. "I don't even *know* him."

"You can spend your whole life with someone, and you still won't know every secret," Alice said. "But there's a point at which you learn enough to know that they're the right one to fill the spaces in your soul that have been waiting for that special someone. When you know, you know. Trust it."

Then, with a wink, she disappeared out the door, shouting at Bella not to double stack the pies.

Stunned, Sofia sank down on the stack of newspapers, hugging Millie to her chest while she processed Alice's words.

She hadn't even thought of trying to rekindle anything with Keegan again.

Yes, she still found him attractive, but there was too much distance between them. And what they'd had wasn't even real. It had been a moment. And now he was a famous celebrity who women would lie, cheat, and steal to have a moment with.

There was no chance. No purpose. No reason. It didn't make sense.

But she couldn't get Alice's words out of her head. Was Alice right? Live a little. Have some fun. Trust the journey.

Millie licked her nose, and Sofia smiled at the puppy. "I've been very serious for a very long time, Millie. I have responsibilities, you know."

Millie waggled her little body and showered her face with puppy kisses that made Sofia start to laugh. "You think I should lighten up and have fun? Let go? Surrender? Trust? I like to be in control. It's not really my nature to let go."

Except it once had been. That time she'd met Keegan, she'd let go. Surrendered. And she'd had the best week of her life, until she'd torn it apart—

"Sascha?" Keegan poked his head in. "You okay?"

Sofia looked at him. Really looked at him. At his blue eyes. At his smile. At the laugh lines around his eyes and mouth. "You look older now."

His brows went up, and he stepped inside and shut the door. "I am older."

"Wisdom looks good on you."

He folded his arms and leaned against the wall, watching her with those eyes that seemed to see everything. "Life looks good on you."

Her belly tightened at the genuineness in his eyes. *He thought she looked good.* "Thank you."

He nodded. "Alice sent me back here to check on you."

"Not surprising. She has some ideas."

He didn't move, but he stiffened ever so slightly. "What kind of ideas?"

Oh...so many. "She thinks I'm too serious, and I need to lighten up. Enjoy the Christmas spirit." *Enjoy you.*

He was quiet for a moment, then he levered himself off the wall and walked across the room. He grabbed a chair, swung it around so it was backwards, then he slung his leg over and sat on it. He braced his arms over the back and leaned over it, a position of raw, relaxed masculinity that made her belly turn over. "I've been wanting a word with you about that."

She raised her brows. "Have you?"

"I have." He rubbed his jaw. "Look, Sascha, I don't know all the details about what you're running from, but I know enough to know that it wasn't easy. All the Harts have been through 'not easy,' and I get it."

She bit her lip, not wanting to talk about it.

But he didn't ask for details. "I want you to know that I will never trap you. I will never take away your freedom. And I will never *ever* use Gabriella as a weapon in our relationship. She's an awesome kid with a soul that deserves to fly."

"She is. She's my world."

"And you are hers. I'll never interfere in that."

Sofia nodded, fighting back the emotion clogging her

throat. Had she been that obvious about her fear of losing her daughter to the glitz of the Hart life? She focused on the puppy on her lap, and as she did, his words floated through her mind. *Our relationship.* What did he mean? As cordial co-parents? As something more?

She didn't care.

But she did. Life was short, too short, and there was no way for her to lie to herself about her reaction to him. She looked at him, testing the waters ever-so-cautiously. "Alice wanted me to know you're a very good man, and I can trust you with Gabby. And..." *with me.* She couldn't bring herself to say it.

He tipped the chair forward, so he was leaning down toward her. "Sascha," he said gently. "Ever since my mom died and I hit the streets and met Brody and the others, my entire life has been about the family we build. I would give my life to protect them, and you and Gabby are in that circle now. Our circle. Whatever you need, whether it's help, space, or whatever."

She looked away, at the Christmas lights blinking on the side porch. "Keegan."

After a moment of waiting for her to continue, he said, "I'm listening."

She looked back at him. "I owe you a lot of explanations—"

"No. You don't owe me anything."

"But—"

"Look," he said. "I'll be honest, I'm burning like hell to find out what happened, and there's a part inside me that feels pretty..." he paused.

"Angry? Furious? Bitter? Like you hate me?"

"Emotional," he supplied, leaving the exact nature of the emotions unspoken. "I still have a lot to process, and to talk about with you, but I'm a survivor, like my siblings, so I recognize and respect what it takes. You did what you had to do to survive, to help your kid thrive. I'm not going to bust on that. It goes against every grain in my body."

She bit her lip and scratched Millie's head, trying to wrap her heart around his words. He sounded like he meant them, but how could he? She'd done too much, gone too far. There was no way he could really forgive her, let alone want to protect her.

"Sascha. Look at me."

Reluctantly, she raised her gaze. "What?"

"It kills me to see that look of fear in your eyes. Fear of me? Of what? How can I take that away so that you can breathe? So you can smile? So you can trust the magic of us being brought together again?"

Magic? She laughed. "Magic? You think it's magic we were brought together? It's a teenager, Keegan."

"No." He shook his head. "There was a reason for it, Sascha. We both know it." He smiled. "You were the free spirit that kept me going all these years. You showed me that I can have fun and be happy even when the shit is raining down around me. And this time, it's my turn to clear the boulders out of your way so you can find that, too."

She stared at him, startled by his words. "Seriously?"

"Yeah." He inched the chair closer. "I've thought about you almost every day for the last seventeen years, Sascha. I wasn't sure if I was making you into something more than you were, but I wasn't." He leaned in. "You're still magical to me, Sascha. Give us this chance."

She blinked. "A chance? Us a chance? Like *us*? You want *us* to have a chance?" She couldn't keep the shock out of her face. "You mean, you and me, together? As a couple?"

"Yes."

"Yes? *Yes*." She stood up and stepped back. "There's no way. We have a daughter. We can't try to date and then have it not work out. How would that work? It wouldn't, because we'd have to keep in touch over Gabby, and it would be awkward and difficult." Her heart started to pound as he stood up, unfolding his long, muscular body from the chair. "You don't even know me. I don't know you. There's no us, and—"

He laid his hand on her cheek.

A gentle touch. Barely there. Brushing over her skin like a caress. But he stole the words from her lips, leaving her in silent, breathless anticipation.

"You remember when I dashed out in front of that truck to heroically save your life?"

His hand was still on her face, warm, gentle, mesmerizing. "I vaguely recall that moment."

"Well, the reason I was there, was because I'd been following you an hour, ever since I saw you talking to a homeless person. You were funny and warm, asking him how his evening was, and making him smile. You lit up the world, and from that moment, I was yours."

Her heart turned over at his confession. "I don't remember that specifically, but I do make sure to talk people who might feel invisible. No one should ever feel invisible." Even now she did it. It mattered to her, and she liked that it mattered to him. "I like people. They have stories. They're interesting."

"And you make them feel like they're interesting." His thumb slid along her cheek, right next to her lips. "You make people feel seen, people who go through life invisible. I was that guy. Invisible. Until you."

She swallowed. "Keegan—"

"I wanted to meet you, but I wasn't about to scare you by approaching you, because I knew that I was nothing more than a rough street kid. So I followed you to make sure you were safe." He gave a half-smile. "And then fate intervened, and I got to meet you." His eyes darkened. "And then I got to know you. And then I got to kiss you. You remember that?"

Oh, Lordy. The way he'd said "kiss" made her remember all sorts of hot and delicious things about him. "By the fountain."

"By the fountain," he agreed. He slid his other hand along her jaw. "I had my hands framing your face this way, as I'd been wanting to do since we met. And then I waited, certain you were going to push me away, expecting you to give me a hard stop. But you didn't."

Her heart was racing now. "No, I didn't," she whispered.

"And what about right now? I've been waiting. Giving you time. You're not pushing me away."

She swallowed. "You can't possibly want to kiss me right now."

"I most definitely want to kiss you right now. How would you feel about that?"

"It doesn't make sense," she whispered, even as she lifted her face to his, searching his blue eyes for answers, for clarity. If she didn't have Millie in her arms, she had a feeling that her arms would already be around his neck, dragging him down to her. "I feel exactly the same way as I did when we met, drawn to you like I can't live without you. *It makes no sense.*"

"It makes perfect sense. Yes, our lives are different than they were back then. We're older. More complicated. But our souls are still the same. We still are who we are, and I've been looking for you for the last seventeen years."

Her heart caught. "That's such a line."

"It's not a line if it's true." He paused. "This is your last chance, Sascha. Your last chance to tell me that you don't want me to kiss you like we were eighteen years old again."

She caught her breath...and said nothing.

And when that heart-warming smile flashed across his handsome face, she knew that he wasn't playing her. "Oh, God," she whispered. "I'm so sure this is a terrible idea."

"All the more reason to do it, seems to me."

Then he drew her in, and kissed her, just like he had so many years ago.

But as perfect as that one had been, this one was a thousand times the magic, the sensations, the perfection.

Maybe it was because of all the years they'd both lived.

Maybe it was because she'd long ago stopped hoping for a kiss like this.

Or maybe it was because he had just become a lot better at kissing.

Regardless, it was a kiss she never wanted to end.

CHAPTER FOURTEEN

KEEGAN KNEW INSTANTLY that his memories had been wrong about Sascha.

Kissing her wasn't as great as he'd recalled for so long.

It was *better*.

Keeping careful not to squish the dog between them, he slid his fingers through Sascha's hair, basking in the silken softness as he angled his head, playing in the kiss, breathing in every sensation of her mouth against his, the warmth of her body, the fire racing through his veins like it had come alive.

Sascha leaned in, one hand on his shoulder, her fingers curling into the fabric of his jacket, holding him tight as she kissed him back.

The kiss went from tentative to searing hot in an instant. He moved in, wrapping his arm around her lower back, pulling her hips against his. The puppy was still between their chests, keeping their upper bodies apart, but it didn't matter. The heat between their hips and lips was electric. Intense. Addicting.

He deepened the kiss, losing himself to the taste of her

lips, the softness, the compassion. This woman was kindness. Warmth. Courage. Everything he'd believed before...he knew it was still there.

The kiss became more intense, more desperate, drawing both of them from their reserved places into an inferno that neither of them wanted to stop. It was as if the same fire that had drawn them together before had been building all this time, just waiting to be unleashed.

He slid his hand down over her butt, and she made a little noise at the back of her throat, a noise of need that seemed to reach right inside him and rip away any last walls he still had. "I need you," he whispered.

"Oh, God." She pulled back at his words, staring at him with desperate need and confusion on her face. "We're not teenagers anymore, Keegan. What are we doing?"

"We're doing what we want."

"I can't do this." She moved back, cradling Millie to her chest like a shield. "Everything is so complicated now. I don't even think I'm capable of trusting a man again, not romantically. And you're Gabby's *dad*. And...God....if we got together, I'd be in the press, and he'd see it..."

Tension gripped Keegan. "Who?" he asked, trying to keep his voice calm and low. "Who would see it?"

She stared at him, and he could see her struggle. She'd been solo for so long, but she was tempted to tell him, to let him help, to break down the walls she'd been living behind for so long. "I can't—"

"Mom! Where are you? We're all done out here—" The door to the storage room flew open, and Gabby poked her head in. She glanced back and forth between them, reading their body language, then her eyes widened. "Holy crap. You guys were making out?"

Sascha's cheeks turned pink. "Gabby—"

"If you guys want to give me a baby sister, I'm cool with

that. Have at it. Let's tighten that bond with the Harts, Mom. Bella and I will wait in the car. Want me to ask her if she has a condom? Wait, no, skip that, right? Complicate the situation. It's good. Bye!" She pulled back and then shut the door with just a little too much enthusiasm.

Sascha sighed and looked at Keegan. "See? Too complicated."

"On the contrary, my darling. It's already complicated. Relatively speaking, us making out really doesn't move the needle that much."

Sascha gave a look that one might give a bratty five-year old. "Kissing moves the needle."

"Not that much in the bad direction, though. I say we make kissing an approved activity and see where we go from there. What do you think?"

She stared at him, then suddenly burst out laughing. "You're certifiably insane, aren't you?"

"Isn't everyone?" Keegan was desperate to figure out the threat hanging over them, but he could feel that the conversation needed to shift right now. He'd broken through her shields, and now he needed to keep her from retreating.

"Probably," she agreed.

He leaned in, his mouth hovering over hers. "So? Kissing is approved? It's honestly a pretty innocuous activity."

She wrinkled her nose. "Kissing you is like lighting the fuse on a nuclear bomb."

He narrowed his eyes. "I'm sure there's a way to interpret that as a compliment, so thank you for that. I assume that's a 'yes?'"

She stared at him for so long that he thought he was going to say no.

But when she spoke, she said instead, "Kissing you makes me feel alive. It's been a long time since I've felt that way."

He grinned. "Me, too. Feels good, right?"

"It does," she agreed.

"We already cheated death, slept together, made a kid, broke up, and then pined over each other for a decade and a half. If we can turn that into something that feels good in the moment..." He shrugged, trying to make it sound as casual as possible, knowing that she didn't want to feel trapped.

She raised her brows. "A little casual, fun kissing? That's all you want?"

"No. It's not all I want," he said honestly, unwilling to lie to her. "But it's a start. See where it goes."

She grimaced. "About the breakup—"

He cut her off with a kiss. A kiss that he poured every bit of convincing into that he could summon. To his delight, she sighed and melted into him, wrapping her free arm around his neck. It wasn't until he was certain that he had her that he finally broke the kiss, but he kept his forehead resting against hers. "I missed you, Sascha. Let's go spread some Christmas cheer. Shall we? Have some fun? Appreciate the gift that brought us together for the holidays?"

She took a breath, then nodded. "Okay."

Okay. Victory seemed to explode through him as he stepped back to let her exit. When he put his hand on her lower back as they walked out, she didn't move away, and she didn't try to stop him.

The door had been opened...and it was staying open.

Yes.

CHAPTER FIFTEEN

SIX HOURS LATER, Sofia knew she was in trouble.

Big. Trouble.

Really. Big. Trouble.

Because she'd just had the best day she could remember having in a long time. Laughter seemed to flow like a waterfall from the Harts, and she and Gabby had been swept up in their zest for life.

They'd visited three more stores, and everyone had been so delighted to see Keegan. People's love for Keegan was genuine and warm, and she could see the impact he'd had on people, simply by bringing them fresh breads he'd made for them.

No. It wasn't the baked goods that made people so happy to see him. It was because he brought a sense of warmth, appreciation, and joy with him. He made everyone he spoke with feel like they mattered, including herself. Including Gabby.

She had a feeling Gabby was falling as hard for Keegan as she was.

Sofia wasn't blind. She knew Keegan was turning the full

force of his charms on both of them, making them both come out of their shells, igniting Sofia with stolen kisses every chance he got.

They'd even stumbled across a group of local townspeople out caroling at one of their stops, and they'd joined in.

Yep, celebrity billionaire Keegan Hart and his equally famous and rich sister had donned borrowed Santa hats and marched around the icy streets belting out Christmas carols with a bunch of strangers who most celebrities probably wouldn't even notice, let alone take an hour to sing with.

He'd even given Gabby a shoulder ride for part of it. A sixteen-year-old getting a shoulder ride! It was adorable and hilarious, and Gabby had been shrieking with laughter.

And now...they were out in the cold night, watching a local Christmas concert right outside the charming lodge they were staying in. The locals had a big bonfire, and Santa was wandering around, handing out candy canes to kids.

Bella and Gabby had taken Millie to get some hot chocolate, and Sofia smiled as she watched them laughing and having such a great time.

Keegan's arms went around her waist, and he rested his chin on her shoulder. "I like hearing your laugh."

She leaned back against him and wrapped her hands around his forearms. "This feels so surreal. This morning, I was at home, stressing about telling Gabby about you, and now we're running around delivering Christmas goodies, and singing Christmas carols, like we're a—" She stopped herself before she could say *family*. They weren't a family. This was a wonderful moment, but that's all it was.

A moment.

"This morning I thought you were dead, and I thought it was possible that I'd had a daughter I'd never met, who was also dead. So yeah, I'd say the day turned out to be a nice surprise." His body was warm and reassuring against her back, his arms snug and protective around her waist.

But she tensed at his reminder of real life.

He swore under his breath and kissed the side of her neck. "Shit. I didn't mean to bring that up. Let's just appreciate this moment. That's what I was trying to say."

"Yeah, okay." But it was too late. The past was with them again. She knew she needed to talk to him, to get everything out of the way before she could even begin to focus on this. But now was not the time. "I'm going to go check on Gabby." She forced herself to step away.

She hurried away without looking back.

KEEGAN WATCHED SASCHA JOG AWAY. No. Not Sascha. *Sofia.*

At first, his instinct had been to call her Sascha, and hers had been as well. To hide in a time when they were teenagers and life was simple. Life hadn't been easy, but it had been simple. Survive. That was it. His only goal. And then, when he'd met this sparkling girl who swept into town and lit up his world, his goal had changed from *survive* to *thrive.*

Sascha was an eighteen-year-old siren who blessed a homeless kid with her teenage love, warmth, and fire.

Sascha was a memory and inspiration that had kept him going for a long time.

Sascha was a bird in flight, her wings always open and soaring, never touching down.

And today...The attraction was still there...more, even. But this wasn't the same as when they were teenagers. They were both older, had lived more, and carried more stories with them.

Sofia was a powerful, intoxicating single mom who had

kept herself and her daughter safe and thriving for almost seventeen years.

Sofia awoke a protective, domestic instinct in him that felt right all the way to his soul.

Sofia made him want to go deep emotionally with her. Not a seven-day interlude of fun and giddiness. He wanted to go all the way, peel back the layers, awaken her sunshine again, and help her with the stories that still held her captive.

As compelling as Sascha had been, Sofia was a thousand times more.

He grinned. More complicated and more challenging, too, but he was up for it. She was worth it. And so was...*Gabby.* Something turned over in his gut as he watched *his daughter* turn around as Sascha...no *Sofia* approached. Sofia put her arm around her daughter and squeezed, and Gabby leaned into her.

The bond between them was so tight. It reminded him of his mom, his memories before she'd died. He knew Sofia and Gabby were special together, that somehow, Sofia had created an incredible bond and life for her daughter, despite whatever trials she'd been facing.

Trials that were still haunting her.

Whatever that danger was, it was still following them, and he'd be damned if he'd let anything happen to them.

Still watching them, he pulled out his phone and called his brother Dylan, who owned a private investigation firm and was very, very good at it.

Dylan answered on the first ring. "Brody told me the news. She's alive, eh?"

"Yep." Keegan noticed that his trio of females was moving away from the hot chocolate stand, and he eased into the crowd to follow them, to make sure that they were never out of sight, and he was always close enough to intervene. "I haven't had the chance to talk to Sofia yet in detail, but as best I can gather, she faked her death and went underground all this time. There's someone she's hiding from, and she's still concerned they could find her and come after her."

Dylan swore under his breath. "Husband?"

"That would be my first guess, but I don't know. Can you do a little work and see what you can dig up on him and anyone who was in her life at the time?"

"Wouldn't it be easier if you just asked her?"

"I have, but I'm not sure she's going to tell me."

"Have you told her the Harts are a bunch of badass protectors that can keep her and Gabby safe from any threat?"

Keegan laughed. "Not in those words. Trying not to scare her into making a run for it."

"Skittish?"

"She's been burned badly. Doesn't want to trust."

Dylan sighed. "I get that. We all get that."

"Yeah, we do. So, you'll take care of that? Follow up with Brody and get his help, too."

"You bet." Dylan paused. "What's it like? Seeing her after all these years?"

Keegan took a breath, trying to find the words. "Like I just came alive."

"Damn. That's awesome. And the kid?"

"She's amazing."

"You think she's yours?"

"She claimed me, and I claimed her, so yeah. Mine." He didn't bother to explain that a paternity test didn't matter. Dylan got it. To the Harts, family had nothing to do with blood ties.

"Fuck. I'm not going to lie. I'm a little jealous. Hope it works out for the three of you. I'd love to see you with a shit-eating grin on your face the next time I see you."

Keegan grinned. "Me, too. Talk later."

"You bet. I'll keep in touch. Let me know if you get any info from her. It would make it easier."

"I know. I'll work on it." Keegan saw Gabby look back for him, Millie zipped in the front of her jacket. When she saw him, her face brightened, and she gestured to him to come catch up.

His heart turned over. "Gotta go. My daughter wants me." *Son of a bitch.* "I can't believe I just said that."

"Absolutely fucking awesome. I love it. Talk later." Dylan hung up.

Keegan shoved his phone in his pocket and broke into a jog, weaving his way around the sparse crowds to catch up. As he neared them, Sofia looked back at him. He shot her a smile, and after a moment, she smiled back before turning away.

Yes. She hadn't shut him out.

Tonight, after Gabby was in bed...tonight, he would get Sofia alone.

Tonight, the walls were going to come down.

CHAPTER SIXTEEN

"MOM!" Several hours later, Gabby flopped down on Sofia's bed, her face glowing. "This was the most amazing day, wasn't it?"

Sofia grinned at her daughter's enthusiasm. "It was pretty fun."

"Keegan is the best. Isn't he nice?"

"He is." Sofia had loved seeing him interact with all his old customers. Their love and affection for him told her so much about who he was, and that her instincts about him were right. Bella clearly adored him, and Sofia adored Bella, so that was more validation.

Keegan Hart was a good man.

"Mom?"

"What's up, sweetie?" Sofia grabbed her flannel pants and camisole from her backpack and headed into the bathroom to get ready for bed.

"Keegan...he seems to totally accept me as his daughter. Do you think he means it?"

Sofia heard the insecurity in her daughter's voice, so she immediately came back to the bed and sat down beside her daughter. "I do, Gabby. To the Harts, family is everything. There is no hesitation there at all. I can see it in the way he looks at you."

Gabby bit her lip. "You really think so? I mean, he didn't even know I existed until today, and now he's willing to go all-in on being my dad? Who does that?"

"The Harts do it. Keegan Hart does it." Sofia smoothed back her daughter's hair, like she used to do when Gabby was little. "You are an incredibly special person, Gabby. Keegan is lucky that you've decided to let him into your world, and he knows it."

Gabby thought about that as she picked at the comforter. "But what about you? Is he mad at you? Because if he's mad at you or mean to you, then I don't want him."

Sofia's throat tightened at her daughter's loyalty, realizing that it must have been weighing on Gabby all day. "He's not mad at me," she said honestly. "He would like to know what happened, but he's not mad. He said that the Harts know all about making tough decisions to survive, and he respects whatever was going on in my life that made me choose the way I did."

Gabby's eyes widened. "He said that?"

"Several times."

"And he meant it?"

"I think he did."

"Wow." Gabby rolled onto her back and stared at the ceiling. "Just, wow."

"I know." Sofia stretched out beside her daughter and clasped her hands behind her head. "Can I ask you something?"

"Sure."

"Would you want to move here with him instead of being in Seattle with me?"

Gabby sat up. "Move here without you?" She looked

horrified. "Is that what this trip is about? You're going to dump me?"

"God, no! I just...I got scared that he was cooler than I was, and you'd want him instead of me."

"Mom! That's the stupidest thing you've ever said, and you've said a lot of stupid things!"

Sofia started laughing through the tears that she hadn't noticed arrive. "I'm not perfect, Gabby. You're my world. I get insecure, too."

"Well, it's still stupid." Gabby curled up next to Sofia, tucking against her side like she did when she was little. "I love you, Mama. Always and forever. To the moon, the stars, the universe and back, times infinity."

Sofia put her arm around her precious baby. "And I love you, Gabriella. Always and forever. To the moon, the stars, the universe, to New York, back to the stars, times infinity."

"Yay." Gabby pressed her face in Sofia's shoulder. "What happens next, Mama?"

"I don't know."

"You think he'll stay in touch?"

"Absolutely."

"Okay." Gabby was quiet for a moment. "Are you going to get back together with him?"

Oh, *Lordy.* "It's too complicated."

"It would be okay with me." Gabby whispered the words.

Sofia smiled. "Because he's rich?"

"No. Because when he says something funny, you smile all the way to your eyes."

Oh. Wow. "I don't usually smile all the way to my eyes?"

Gabby shrugged. "Sometimes, but not like when he says something funny. It's just different." She cocked her head. "You look really beautiful when you're listening to him. Like... I don't know."

Gabby's observation stunned Sofia. The teenager was

sixteen, an age notorious for noticing nothing but their own lives, and certainly not their parents. "Wow. That's surprisingly deep for a sixteen-year-old."

Gabby grinned. "I know, right? Don't get used to it. I'll probably steal your car tomorrow or something, and everything will be back in line again."

Sofia laughed. "We can only hope, but you're never driving again."

"Of course not. I definitely believe you."

"I'm serious. I'm going to become one of those hardcore parents, now that you've proven yourself untrustworthy."

Gabby rolled her eyes. "There's nothing hardcore about you, Mom. You don't even believe the word "rules" should have been invented—"

At that moment, Sofia's phone rang. They both looked down, and Gabby grinned when Keegan's name flashed on her screen. "He probably wants to invite you for a private dessert."

Sofia rolled her eyes back at her daughter. "Probably not, and either way, I'm staying here with you. Girl time—"

"No. You need to talk to him." Gabby grabbed the phone and answered it. "Hi Keegan, it's Gabby. My mom's in the bathroom. What's up?"

Sofia rolled onto her back and stared at the ceiling, listening to the joy in her daughter's voice. The sassiness. The snarkiness. Keegan made Gabby feel safe enough to be sassy to him. She appreciated that so much.

"Sure. That's fine," Gabby said. "Ten minutes? I'll send her down."

"What?" Sofia sat up abruptly, shaking her head and waving her hands in the universal sign for "No freaking way!"

Gabby hung up and grinned at her. "He'll meet you in the bar. He has a window seat in the back."

Sofia held up her pajamas. "Too late. I'm getting ready for

girls' night. We'll watch a movie—" She paused at the reproachful look on her daughter's face. "What?"

"You're avoiding. You didn't tell him about me sixteen years ago, and now you're still not going to talk to him? What's so scary about him? Because if he's scary, you need to tell me."

Realization settled deep in Sofia's bones. Her daughter was right. She did need to face Keegan, a conversation that was a decade and a half overdue, both for her sake and her daughter's. And for Keegan's. For all of them. "You'll be okay? I won't be long."

"I'll be fine. Take as long as you want. This hotel is gorgeous, and I can stream any service from their television. I'm going to binge watch and order room service until you're broke, and you'll have to pay for it all because of the guilt you feel at depriving me and Keegan of a lifetime together." Gabby waved her off. "Go, go. Leave me to milk your guilty conscience to the maximum extent I can."

Ah...guilt. "That's so rude to try to make me feel guilty."

"It's not rude. It's my job as a teenager to make you a better person." Gabby grinned. "Have fun."

"Fun?"

"Yeah, remember that? We had some today. It's not a bad way to live."

Sofia let out her breath and stood up, leaving her pajamas on the bed. "I can be fun."

Gabby grinned. "I know. I'm just mocking you because you're stalling."

"I'm not stalling."

"No?"

Crap. Gabby was right. She was totally stalling. "Okay, I'm going." She grabbed her room key and her phone, and slid both of them in her pocket. "If you need anything—"

"I'm good. Go."

"Right. Okay. Bye." Sofia put her hand on the doorknob—

"Wait!"

"What?"

"You're going to wear that? What about makeup? Something a little sexier?"

Oh, God. She wanted to rush back over there and freshen up, but that would be trying too hard. Asking for what she wasn't sure she wanted. "I am what I am, Gabby. I can't fake that."

"You could try—"

"Not this time." She blew her daughter a kiss and headed out into the hall before she could change her mind and bail from her first private moment with the man who had turned her world upside down so many years ago...and still did.

CHAPTER SEVENTEEN

KEEGAN SHIFTED RESTLESSLY in the booth, watching the door to the pub. Each time it opened, he tensed...and then sat back in disappointment when he saw it wasn't Sofia.

Would she come?

He'd chosen a booth by the windows, with a view over the horizon. The storm had moved on, and the sky was bright with stars and the moon. The ice made all the trees and earth sparkle, as if someone had painted it with magic...

The door opened again, and this time, it was her.

Keegan's heart started racing as she scanned the room, looking for him. When her gaze fell on him, he grinned and stood up.

Her returning smile was instant, instinctive, he suspected.

He felt like he was holding his breath as she made her way across the pub, worried that she was there to tell him that she wasn't going to stay. But when she neared, all he got from her was a nervous smile. "Hi."

Relief rushed through him. "Hey."

She didn't sit down. She was restless. "Sit here?"

"Or we can walk outside? It's cold but beautiful."

She looked out the window. "It's breathtaking."

"It is. That's why I chose this seat."

"I didn't bring a coat."

"We have a bunch in the truck. We can grab one and then just wander around." He suddenly wanted to be outside with her, not sitting with a table between them. "Cool?"

She nodded. "Okay."

Words were sparse as he led the way through the adorable pub, down the hall, and to his truck. He went through the stash Bella had put in the back, and fleeces and hat for both of them. Within moments, they were both wrapped up and warm.

"There's a cool lookout point up here." Keegan led the way through the parking lot, and down a little trail that had been treated with sand to deal with the ice. They made it down the trail to a little precipice with a covered swing that sat perched on the edge.

Sofia let out a little gasp. "How did you know this was here?"

"I always stay at this hotel when I do this run. I found this spot on my second time here. It's really glorious in the summer as well." He put one of the blankets on the bench of the two-person swing that was more like a wicker love nest than a swing. "Have a seat."

Sofia didn't hesitate. She sat right down, leaving enough space for him.

He sat next to her, then draped another blanket across their laps. There was enough room that they weren't touching, but he was viscerally aware of how close she was. He pushed off with his feet, and the swing began to move gently.

"It's like heaven up here," Sofia said. "The ice storm is so gorgeous in the moonlight."

"It is," he agreed. "It's like an ice kingdom."

For a long moment, neither of them spoke. He felt

consumed by the moment, of sitting there with her. "You remember the fountain?"

She didn't look over. "You mean, when we sat on the wall and dangled our feet in it, until security chased us off?"

"Yeah."

"Don't remember that."

He laughed, and she grinned, finally looking over at him. "Thank you for being so nice to Gabby."

"You don't need to thank me. It's automatic." He paused for a moment. "Is that why you didn't tell me? Because you thought I'd be an asshole about it? About her?"

Sofia sighed, pulled her knees to her chest, and wrapped her arms around them, in a defensive, protective position, making herself small.

Shit. He hated seeing her like that. "Sofia?"

She turned her head sharply. "You called me Sofia. Not Sascha."

He nodded. "I'm beginning to see you as Sofia now. Sascha was a teenager. You're more than that now. You're a mom, a survivor, smart, protective, and strong. So, Sofia."

She bit her lip. "Sascha is the one you fell for, right? So that means that you're not interested? I mean, that's fine, I'm not either—"

"Hey." He put his hand on her arm. "It was a compliment. And do you really want to open that door of whether I'm interested in you? Because I will walk right through it, but I'm not sure you're ready for it." He kept his voice low, as non-threatening as possible, but he also let her hear the undercurrent in his voice, that a lack of interest was not his current mental state.

She looked at him, and her eyes widened when she saw the expression on his face. "Oh."

He grinned. "Yeah. Oh."

She looked back across the horizon, but a small smile was playing at the corners of her mouth. "Okay."

His smile widened. She hadn't told him to back off. The door was open, and he was going to walk through...just as soon as they got through this conversation. "Talk to me, Sofia. What happened that night?"

She slanted a glance at him. "You remember that night?"

Did he remember? "I recall very clearly going back to your hotel room and making love four times over the course of the night. It was incredible. I was all in, and I told you I loved you. You said you loved me. Then, in the morning, you woke up..." He paused, trying to figure out the best way to say it.

"On a rampage of meanness?"

He inclined his head. "I was going to say losing your shit, but yeah, that works. Then you kicked me out, and when I went back a few hours later, you had packed up your stuff and left. You'd bribed the hotel owner not to tell me anything, because you told him you feared for your life and you were on the run from me. He actually called the cops on me, and Brody had to bail me out." He didn't go into what had happened when he'd gotten pulled back into the system that he'd run from as a foster kid. It had taken Brody months to get him extricated from their claws again.

The memories made him tense, and he took a breath, unwilling to hold onto an experience from so long ago.

She looked at him sharply. "Oh, God. I'm sorry. I didn't mean that. I just...he assumed...and I let him."

"So, you didn't think I was going to hurt you? That you had to fear for your safety around me?" He had to ask it. The thought had weighed on him all this time, wondering if he'd done something to make her feel scared.

Sofia spun toward him and grabbed his arm. "No, God. No. Keegan. I promise you, I'd never felt so safe in my life. I loved being with you. I loved our night together. I loved everything about it. I just, I was so afraid that I'd stay with you if I had the chance, so I had to do whatever it took to get free before I was trapped."

"Trapped," he repeated. "There's that word again. If you thought so highly of me, why would you fear I'd trap you?" But even as he asked it, some of the weight that had been on his shoulders for a decade and a half faded away. *She hadn't actually been afraid of him.*

Jesus. The relief was staggering.

"No. I would trap myself." She tossed the blanket aside and got up, pacing restlessly away from him before she turned to face him. "My dad was a bad guy," she said. "My mom left him when I was a teenager, but his shadow was always over us."

Fuck. He didn't like that at all. "Is still alive?" Was he the one she was running from?

"I don't know." She shrugged. "But all my mom wanted for me was to go to college. To have a career where I earned enough money to be independent. To never have to be with a man because I couldn't afford to take care of myself."

He nodded. "I agree."

"I had a full ride to Harvard, and I was on my way there when you and I met. I was driving cross country, but I didn't want to go." She looked at him. "I didn't want to go east. I didn't want to be a part of an old, traditional institution. But my mom had just died, and I'd promised her. I couldn't let her down."

He swore under his breath. "I'm so sorry you lost her."

Sofia nodded. "I had to keep my promise, but you..." She gestured at him. "You were so tempting. You lived this life of freedom and no rules. I wanted to stay with you, Keegan."

His gut turned over. "Really?"

She nodded. "But for what? You were a homeless runaway

living under a bridge. I had a full ride at college and a promise to my mom. I owed it to her to make a better choice than that. So, I left the only way I knew how, and that was to try to destroy what we had." The guilt hit Sofia hard and deep. She'd forgotten how it had felt that night. "I thought I was going to break both of us," she whispered. "I'm so sorry. I didn't mean it. I just... I couldn't trap myself."

Keegan understood now. The trap hadn't been him. It had been her. "I get it."

"Do you?"

He laughed softly. "Fuck, Sofia, I didn't want to live under a bridge either. I never would have wanted you to give that up for me. I would have gone with you rather than let you stay, if you'd tried to make that choice."

She stared at him. "Gone with me?"

"Yeah, I had nothing there. I mean, yeah, I had Brody and the others, but they weren't my family yet. I had shut them out."

"You would have *gone with me*?"

He frowned. "Is that bad?"

"Just...God..." She threw up her hands. "I never even thought of that. All this time, and I never even thought you'd go with me. My experience with my mom and dad was that it was always one-sided, that the woman always had to give it all up. You would have *gone with me*?"

Keegan stood up and caught her shoulder as she started to spin away. "Sofia," he said softly. "I say that now, but I was a stupid eighteen-year-old hoodlum back then. Who knows what I would have done?"

She stared at him, but didn't try to pull away. "When I found out I was pregnant, I was two months into college. I freaked. I didn't know how to find you, and you were homeless, right?"

He nodded. "I was." He was suddenly tense, waiting to hear about that moment that could have changed everything.

"I had to do better for my daughter than my mom had done for me. She married a guy who never amounted to anything, and he nearly broke us both."

He ground his jaw, but what could he say? That was who he'd been back then.

She looked down at their joined hands. "I was trying to be brave, but I was scared. I was in the hospital alone after Gabby was born, and I met a guy who was there, visiting a friend of his who had also given birth. He was everything my mom had dreamed I'd marry: rich, attractive, connected, nice." She looked at him. "And he wanted me and Gabby. I was stunned. He swept me off my feet, and within six months, we were married, and I'd quit school to raise Gabby."

God, she still remembered that whirlwind time, the magic feeling that life had finally given her the dreams she'd always had. That things had finally worked out for her.

Keegan was watching her, an inscrutable expression on his face. "What happened?"

"He came home from work late and drunk, and he hit me." Involuntarily, she touched her cheek remembering the pain of that strike.

Keegan closed his eyes. "Son of a bitch."

"And then he threatened to hurt Gabby if I told anyone or tried to leave."

"Bastard. How long did you stay?"

She grinned. "My mom taught me how to be strong and how to protect my kid. So, the next day, I went to see a lawyer, a woman, who was very good and very helpful. A week later, when he was on a business trip, I went to the bank and got a bunch of cash, loaded the car, and Gabby and I ran away."

"Nice. You started making plans immediately. Gabby's lucky to have you."

She flashed a smile at him. "Well, honestly, it took a while to stop feeling guilty that I'd believed in him for as long as I did, but I read a lot of self-help books and listened to podcasts, until I realized that I wasn't the issue there."

"Absolutely correct on that." He raised his brows. "You faked your death?"

She nodded. "I had to. He would have hunted us down, I had no doubt. So, Eliana, my lawyer—"

The name startled him. "Eliana? Eliana Tiernan?"

She looked at him in surprise. "Yes. You know her?"

"Yeah, I do. She works with our family a lot, and my brother Dylan has a crush on her. She specializes in helping women break free of bad prenuptial agreements."

"Oh, she does a lot more than that. She got me and Gabby new identities, helped us set up a new account with the money I'd taken, and got all the legalities arranged for me to start our new life."

Damn. He was impressed. "I always knew she was a badass, but not at that level."

Sofia nodded. "I'd heard of her when my mom and I had been at shelters. Women talk about her. She wouldn't even take any of my money. She wanted me to have it all to take care of myself and Gabby."

He'd known Eliana worked pro bono for the clients that needed her services for free, which is why the Harts had created a charitable fund for her to draw from, but *hell*. Small freaking world. "I'm glad you had her."

"Me, too. She saved our lives, I'm sure of it."

"But you worry he'll still come after you?"

She nodded. "He came to see Eliana a few years ago. Apparently, he somehow tracked us to her. He threatened her, but she wouldn't budge. She was able to send a message to me to be careful, that he was still looking for us." She put her hands on her hips and looked up at Keegan. "If something happens to me, you'll take Gabby, right? She'll always have your family if he finds me?"

Oh, hell. "He won't find you."

"He might. He has a lot of resources." She shrugged. "I don't choose men well," she said. "My dad was terrible, and my mom never really escaped his influence, even though she left him when I was twelve. And then I married a monster. After that, I just wanted my freedom, to never be trapped, to never let a man be able to trap me, or Gabby."

He nodded. "I get that." Yeah, he got that. Some of his siblings had come from very rough family situations.

"I didn't know how to find you when I first left," she said. "But one day, I was at the grocery store, and I saw your picture on one of those tabloid covers. I thought it was a joke, and then I read the article, and I knew it was you. I started seeing you and your family on all the covers everywhere. Rich, powerful, attractive...which made you terrifying to me."

"Because of your ex."

She nodded. "I didn't want your money or your attention. I just wanted to live my little life, but I always felt guilty. A what if? I read every article about you, and everything I read made you and your family sound like such good people. I worried I'd made a mistake, but it was too late, right? Too late to show up with a teenager, a story, and an apology. Plus, what if I were wrong, and you were like him? So, I let it be, until Gabby forced me to pay up on a promise I'd made years ago, and tell her who her biological dad was." She shrugged. "I know, it's not much of a story or an excuse, but it's what it is."

"No." Keegan took her hands and brought them to his mouth, where he pressed a kiss to her knuckles, stunning her into silence. "It's a story of a woman who was strong enough to protect her baby and herself. I get it. Every Hart has spent half their life looking over their shoulder for threats from their old life. We've all had to make choices that we wish we hadn't had to make, but survival wins every time. You do what you need to do."

She stared at him, then sudden tears filled her eyes. "You mean that."

"I do." He paused, thinking. "Is your ex-husband's name on Gabby's birth certificate?"

Sofia shook her head. "I never put it on. We'd just met when she was born, so obviously I didn't at that point. Things unraveled so quickly in our marriage that I knew I wouldn't change it then. I've always been so grateful for that. The little blessings in life, right?"

"So, it's blank?"

She laughed softly. "Don't worry. I didn't put your name on it."

"I want to be on it."

Her heart jumped. *"What?"*

Keegan held up his hands. "I'm not trying to scare you or take over. I was simply thinking that if my name is on Gabby's birth certificate, she's protected from him legally. I want to claim her legally as my daughter, as a Hart."

Sofia felt the truth of his words, his need to protect and nurture, and suddenly, emotions she'd kept bottled up for so many years seemed to flood out of her. The shame. The guilt. "God, Keegan, I'm sorry I didn't tell you. I—"

"No." He cut her off. "Never apologize for being you and living your life. Never."

"Aren't you mad?" She almost shouted the question through her tears, almost wanting him to get angry, to treat her the way she sometimes felt she should be treated.

"Mad?" With a sigh, he caught her wrists, and drew their joined hands to his chest. "Sofia, look at the story you just told me from an outsider's point of view. Who on earth would judge you for that, other than yourself?"

His hands felt so good and warm surrounding hers. Like he was pouring heat into the icicles trying to grip her hands. "I—"

"No one. No one would judge you. Especially not me, because I get it."

"But you missed sixteen years with Gabby—"

He nodded. "I'm not going to lie that I'm going to have to process that loss, because it's real. As is the fact I missed sixteen years with you. I'm going to wonder what I could have done back then to show you that I was a good guy, because even back then, I would have stood by you both and protected you." He pressed a kiss to her knuckles. "But angry? No. Never."

She searched his face and saw no anger in his eyes. Just honest integrity. Pain. Yes, pain was in there too. Fresh tears trickled out of her eyes, and she pressed her hands to his cheeks. "I will always wonder if Gabby would have been more whole if I'd trusted you," she whispered. "If she'd had a dad in her life instead of just me."

"Gabby seems pretty freaking awesome to me."

She smiled, some of the tightness around her chest easing. "She is. Completely."

He took a breath. "Besides, we can't change the past."

"No."

"We have only this moment, and the future ones."

She nodded silently, caught in the intensity of his gaze.

"She has me now. As a dad, and as a protector." He paused. "And you have me, too."

"I don't want—"

"I know." And he kissed her anyway.

CHAPTER EIGHTEEN

WHEN KEEGAN FELT Sofia melt into him, something inside him seemed to come alive.

He framed her face with his hands and angled his head, deepening the kiss, coaxing her to life. He was so careful, grimly aware now of her past and her valid fear of men and trusting herself with a guy.

He wanted to give her space from him...but at the same time, he wanted to give her the gift of realizing she could trust him.

She leaned into him, gripping the front of his jacket as she kissed him back. The electric spark was still there, visceral and alive, ensnaring him in the magic of her touch and her lips.

Desire and need began to pulse through him, and he deepened the kiss, surrendering to the power of her soul calling to him. He kept a tight rein on himself, though, unwilling to let himself lose control, refusing to put his needs before his awareness of her response.

But she didn't pull back. In fact, she kissed him more

deeply, giving him all she was, releasing the walls she'd built between them.

With a low groan, Keegan slid his hands to her hips, drawing her against him. She came willingly, and suddenly, the kiss took on a power of its own, catapulting him back into those same sensations of when he was eighteen and falling hard and fast for the free-spirited whirlwind that had blown into his life.

He was falling again. Hard. Fast. He knew it didn't make sense. They had so much to unpack...but at the same time, their conversation had already loosened the stranglehold on their connection.

He understood her.

He admired her.

He was completely sucked into her spell.

And he knew that with her background, he might never convince her to give him a chance and trust him. She might walk away and disappear again. Swearing, he realized he needed to pause what happening between them. He didn't want to push too hard and make her want to run. He had to give her space.

"I want to go back to your room," she whispered against his mouth. "Can we go back there?"

He pulled back, shocked by her words. "What?"

Her cheeks turned red. "Never mind. Forget it. I can't believe I just said that." She took a breath. "Okay, so we're good, then? Over the past and all that? I forgot to tell you that I have a Christmas party at my store on Monday, so I really can't stay for the Hart party tomorrow. We'll have to grab my car and head back. Cool? Okay, bye." Then she turned and started running back to the hotel.

What.

The.

Heck.

"Sofia!" He broke into a jog, but she didn't look back or slow down.

In fact, she was already in the door by the time he caught up to her. He reached for her wrist, but she jerked it out of his grasp and kept running. "Go away, Keegan. Forget it. Just go."

He swore under his breath, sprinted past her, then stopped in front of her, blocking the hallway. He held up his hands in surrender when she stopped. "Sascha. I just want to talk."

"No." She backed up. "Look, I literally was just willing to have sex with you. The last time I did that, I wound up with a baby, who I love, yes, but it was also a complete shitshow of my life. I'm attracted to you. So what? I'm a freaking grown woman, and I'm not going to go jump into bed with you because I can't help myself. I don't even do that. Just with you, and you are—" She cut herself off.

"I'm what?" He was glad he had her talking, but he wasn't feeling all that optimistic about how she was was feeling about him.

"You're powerful. Rich. Famous. You're my kid's dad, and she loves you. You're standing on the precipice of having total control over my life, and that's without me even falling in love with you again. What the hell am I thinking? Asking you to go to bed with me? I'm not that much of an idiot. I really am not."

Shock ripped through him. "You're falling in love with me?"

"No. I said I'm *not* going to make that mistake again. Not with you. Not with anyone. I'm just not—"

At that moment, they both heard a snicker. They spun in time to see a pair of teenage boys standing there recording them with their phone.

Sofia sucked in her breath.

Oh, shit. Keegan headed toward them. "I'm going to need you guys to delete that right now."

The boy with the phone held it up, continuing to film as Keegan approached. "Can I have your autograph?"

Behind him, he heard Sofia's footsteps as she sprinted down the hall. He wanted to go after her, but it was more important that he keep that video off the internet. "Guys. You need to stop recording." His instinct was to lunge for them and rip the phone out of his hand, but the Harts prided themselves on being better than that.

They didn't stop recording. "Yes, that's right," the teenager said, "we're live streaming Keegan Heart and his girlfriend from Moose Lodge in Washington. Does anyone know who she is? Please put her name in the comments, if you do!"

Urgency coursed through him. *Fuck it.* Keegan leapt forward and snatched the phone from the guy's hand. He immediately stopped the video, and hit delete, but not before he saw there were already two hundred comments. He swore. "How long were you videoing us for?"

The teenager had the decency to look embarrassed. "Since you guys came out into the hall."

Shit. Keegan looked down at the phone, then swore. "You have over ten million followers?"

"Yeah. I'm AceThree on—"

"I don't care." Keegan shut the phone off. "Post anything about her again, and my lawyers will be on you so fast you won't know what hit you." As a public person, he had limited resources available to stop the streams, but it was different with Sofia.

"Sure." The kid sounded completely unbelievable. "Give me my phone back. You can't keep it. Who is she to you?"

Keegan ground his jaw, trying to decide the right way to handle this. After a moment, he decided on honesty. "That woman is in danger. If the wrong person sees your video and figures out where she is, she could be in trouble. I'll do a video for you if you want, but you gotta keep her off your feed. Get it?" He let his urgency show, trusting that the kid was a decent kid.

Sure enough, his eyes widened. "No shit?"

"No shit."

"How much danger?"

"I'm trying to figure that out exactly, but I would appreciate it if you kept everything about her offline."

The teenager nodded. "Yeah, sure." Then he grinned. "About that video of you?"

Keegan sighed. He needed to go after Sofia, but ensuring her physical safety came first. "Yeah, you got five minutes."

The kid's face lit up. "Cool." He unlocked his phone. "Let's do it."

CHAPTER NINETEEN

JUST AROUND THE CORNER, Sofia closed her eyes and leaned her head back against the wall, listening as Keegan started doing the interview with the teenager.

He'd handled it perfectly, getting the video offline, but still being a good guy.

Her ex would not have been nice to the boy in that situation, which showed that Keegan was different.

She knew he was different.

But her old instincts wouldn't let her believe it.

She'd freaked out and lost her mind when she'd invited herself back to Keegan's room. Scared herself so badly that she'd literally gone into panic mode and run for her life.

Slowly, she slid down the wall and sat on the carpet, pulling her knees to her chest as she listened to the interview. The kid was clearly in awe of Keegan, but Keegan was warm and funny, giving him his full attention, not a half-hearted interview that he didn't want to do.

Keegan talked about Christmas with his family, about their traditions, and their annual party. He told the boy he was delivering Hart's Bakery items to his local customers. His voice was full of such pride and warmth as he talked about Alice and her wonderful store, and the others they'd visited today.

Sofia smiled as she listened to Keegan describe each store, and what they brought that was so special to the Christmas season. By the time he finished, she was ready to go back to each store and live there.

Keegan might be a billionaire celebrity, but in his heart, he was a regular cowboy who loved the local folk, rescued horses, and protected those he cared about. He was still the teenage runway who had lost his mom in an accident and had fought to find his place in the world after society had let him down...a man who somehow had never let life chip away at the goodness that defined him.

She closed her eyes, listening to the sound of his voice, letting it wrap around and soothe the fear from her body. Without his attention on her, without having to worry about how she was feeling about him, it was safe to let his presence fill her heart with the peace and warmth that was him.

God, what was she going to do?

She realized that the reason she'd freaked out and run was because she was falling for him hard, just like before.

It was less than a day, and he seemed to consume her simply with his presence.

Was she brilliantly insightful that he was her match? Or just a foolish woman falling for a handsome knight who was willing to rescue her?

"Sofia?"

She opened her eyes to see Keegan crouching in front of her, his brow furrowed with concern. "Did you ever get married, Keegan? Are you in a relationship now?" She couldn't believe she'd never asked him that before having fantasies about him.

He sat down across from her and leaned against the wall,

so his feet were touching hers. "I was engaged until a couple months ago."

"A couple *months*?" Suddenly, the same fear was back, that he was a player. "What happened?"

He shrugged. "I found out that she was in love with someone else. She wanted to marry Keegan Hart for the bling, but she had no intention of giving up her relationship with the guy she actually loved."

"Ouch."

"Yeah." He rested his forearms on his knees, watching her. "A couple of my siblings have tried to find someone, but other than Brody and Tatum, it's been tough. People see us as Harts, not as people. It's not worth it to try to filter out who is who anymore. At least not for me."

She bit her lip. "So, you have trust issues as well, then."

"I do. We all do."

She nodded. "I get that."

He rubbed his jaw. "Here's the thing, Sofia. You knew me before I was the guy that people care about. Our past...it's just us. It's not glamour or fame. It was simply us, and it was real. Right?"

"Yes," she whispered her answer.

"And when you found out about me, who I was, you never came after me. Not for my money. Not for a payoff. Not for anything. You just stayed away."

Understanding began to dawn. "So, that actually makes you trust me more, then?"

"Yeah." He held out his hand to her.

After a brief hesitation, she leaned forward and put her hand in his. His palm was rough and calloused, a man who, despite his money, still got out and lived life. He didn't close his hand around hers. He just kept his hand open, watching their fingers rest against each other. "You're both Sascha and

Sofia to me," he said quietly. "I fell in love with Sascha, but Sofia is pretty amazing, too."

She watched their hands together, too. Her skin was considerably darker than his, contrasted shades that somehow seemed to become whole when they were together, just like before.

"Sitting on the floor in a hallway with you feels like old times."

He grinned. "We had no house to stay in. No hotel until that last night."

"Nope." She closed her fingers, holding onto his hand, but he didn't grip her back. He kept his hand loose and relaxed. "Sorry I freaked out."

"Totally understandable. Sorry about the video."

She looked up at him. "Did it go online?"

"Yep. Live streaming. He had two hundred comments already."

A familiar tension settled in her gut. "He might see it."

"Then we need to make plans."

She bit her lip. "I could just go home—"

"No." His fingers closed around hers this time. "Don't hide again, Sofia. You've been hiding for sixteen years, and we all lost out. Whether you choose to stay with me or not is irrelevant. Just don't hide again. Don't run. I'm powerful and so is my family. Use that power to your advantage. Fight this time. You have an army behind you."

Oh, God. "There are so many things in that little speech that I want to respond to." Choose to stay with him? Was he asking her to stay with him? To try again? To see what happened? She couldn't. Could she?

"I want to hear them all eventually, but right now, I need to hear that you're not going to disappear in the middle of the night again." He searched her face. "Don't run from me again, Sofia. Promise me that."

She met his gaze. "I can't promise you anything. I won't. That traps me."

Tension flickered in his jaw. "Will you consider it?"

She let out her breath. The idea of no longer having to look over her shoulder was so tempting, almost surreal. "If there is a way to make it so Gabby never has to be afraid again, I would do it." If she kept herself focused on what was right for her daughter, then she knew she could trust her choices.

He nodded. "My family and I can do that." He paused. "Sofia, we can make sure that neither of you need to worry that something bad is going to happen to you."

Sudden tears flooded Sofia's eyes, and emotion seemed to seize her throat. "For sixteen years, I have lived in fear that if something happened to me, if he found me, then there would be no one to protect her, to take care of her. My business partner, Jocie, is who would take her, but she doesn't have the resources to hide from him. I just... It's haunted me every minute of every day and—" She stopped, unable to talk past the emotion.

As a mom, there was literally nothing that mattered more than her daughter's well-being. The thought of her ex finding them and killing her had been terrifying. But equally scary had been the worry that if she ever got in an accident or had anything else happen to her that left Gabby alone. "It's hard to be a single parent with no family," she whispered. "It's terrifying, the 'what ifs' that can get you."

"I get it. I was the kid of a single mom with no family. I know what happens when the parent dies."

She heard the emotion in his voice and looked at him. "Oh, Keegan."

He shrugged it off. "That's why I will do whatever it takes to make sure both of you are safe. I'm not trying to trap you. I'm trying to protect you from what happened to me."

And that was it. The moment she knew she could trust him with what mattered most: her baby girl's well-being. With tears trickling down her cheeks, she leaned forward, put her hands on Keegan's face, and kissed him.

Without fear.

Without hesitation.

Just with an open heart and a need to connect with this gift that the universe had given her...twice.

Keegan immediately grabbed her around the waist and pulled her toward him. She went willingly, climbing into his arms and onto his lap. She sank down on him, her knees on either side of his hips, kissing him with all the emotions that had been pent up inside her for so long.

She wasn't afraid. For the first time in so long, the shadow of fear wasn't hovering at the edge of her mind.

Keegan locked his arms around her waist, kissing her with the same commitment coursing through her. He felt so good against her. Hard. Strong. Muscled. Solid.

She couldn't get enough of him. She leaned into him, locking her arms around his neck, meeting his kisses with the same urgency that he was tapping into.

He swore suddenly. "Too many potential cameras around. I'm not exposing you like this."

Before she could react, he locked his arms around her and surged to his feet.

"You can put me down—"

"Nope. Can't. You might run away." He got a better grip on her, then headed down the hall with a purposeful stride. When they got into the elevator and the door slid shut behind him, he started kissing her again.

Hot.

Delicious.

Getting more intense by the second.

By the time the elevator opened, they were both breathing hard.

He didn't hesitate. He didn't ask. He simply headed straight down the hall and unlocked a door. "We'll have to be quiet," he whispered. "Gabby's right across the hall."

She looked over his shoulder as he carried her into his room and saw her room number. "You booked us across the hall from you?"

"You were afraid of someone hurting you. Was there even a chance I'd stay anywhere except within earshot of you, in case you needed me?" As he spoke, he pushed the door shut, locked it, then carried her to the bed. "I'm a protector, sweetheart. Always have been. Always will be."

Oh, le swoon...

He laid her on the bed and then lowered himself on top of her, nibbling at her neck as he used one hand to unlace her boots. "Leave no child or woman unprotected," he murmured, "at least to the extent we can."

This was the man she'd been so afraid of for so long? *This man?* "You had me at protector."

He laughed, his voice a rich, deep, laugh. Then he started kissing her again, and she forgot about things like room numbers and swooning. All she could focus on was the feeling of being in Keegan's arms again, after so many years.

Being with him was everything she'd remembered, and so much more. Before, their connection had been instant and vibrant, but it had also been the innocence of two ungrounded teenagers trying to cling to a moment of wonder in the midst of hardship.

This time, it was so much more, so much deeper. When he pulled her shirt over her head and pressed a kiss to the swell of her breast, it felt as if her soul had come home, settling happily and purposefully into his safekeeping.

His body felt magical against hers. Hard. Muscled. Strong.

As more and more clothes kept disappearing, and more and more skin-to-skin contact happened, she felt like she'd fallen into an oasis of warmth and sizzling electricity.

He kissed his way down her belly, his hands splayed on her bare hips, a caress that invited her to melt into his grasp... which she did. Complete surrender. Total trust. She hadn't let go so completely in years, maybe ever. She became one with the moment, with the intimacy, with the heat leaping back and forth between them.

She heard the crinkle of a foil wrapper, and then he was moving over her. They met gazes as he slipped inside her, an easy, perfect fit that made her light up from the inside out.

He smiled, tangling his fingers in her hair as he gazed down at her, such warmth in his eyes. "The look on your face right now is enough to melt even the hardest heart, and my heart is already soft for you."

She grinned back at him, sliding her hands over his muscled chest. "Last time we were together, you weren't this solid."

"You didn't have all these curves either, so I think we both filled in nicely, don't you?" He began to move, eliciting sensations inside her that she hadn't felt in a very long time.

"Oh, God. Yes. I'm definitely the lucky one—"

"No." He paused. "Don't discredit yourself. You're incredible, and I want you to feel that. To know it."

A warm feeling came over her at his urgency, and she couldn't help but smile. "You're kind of adorable."

He laughed, a deep, rich laugh of pure joy. "Thanks. Me and Millie. And I left her with Bella, by the way. I didn't want her to be alone while you and I were talking."

Thoughtful and adorable? He was too much. But she'd take it—

He bent down and kissed her again, and this time it was a kiss meant to tantalize and tease, to draw her irrevocably into the movement of his hips. She surrendered without hesitation, allowing herself to breathe in the beauty of being with him. When they were teenagers, it had been hot and wild, but clouded with her guilt about how much she wanted to abandon college and stay with him. Dragged down by her own insecurities.

So, this time, she let it all go. She let it be wonderful. She let it feel amazing. She let herself love every second of being with him. And most of all, she let herself feel the warmth and kindness and safety of Keegan himself.

Surrendering to the good emotions changed everything about the moment. It took on an energy of gloriousness, of positivity, of healing. Yes, that was it. *Healing.* The healing power of love, both of the soul and the body.

And when the moment took her over the edge, she let go. He surrendered at the same moment, and they clung to each other, holding on to the moment, to each other, to the purity of two souls coming back to find each other to finish a story that had barely gotten started.

CHAPTER TWENTY

SOFIA NESTLED DEEPER AGAINST KEEGAN, closing her eyes to breathe him in. "I don't want to move," she whispered.

He kissed the top of her head. "Me either."

She could feel his heart beating against her cheek, where she was resting her face against his chest. She knew she had only a few minutes before she needed to head back across the hall to be with Gabby, but for these few moments, she wanted to be fully present, to try to start to build the connection that they'd never had time to explore. "My partner in my store ordered Hart's Bakery for our Christmas party."

He grunted, trailing his fingers lightly across her lower back. "You can get it free. Family discount."

She smiled. "I just wanted to say congrats on the bakery. I remember how it was your dream, even back then."

Keegan was quiet, just running his fingers over her back.

She frowned. "Keegan?"

"I appreciate the kind words. Thanks."

Her frown deepened at his formal response, and she sat up, so she could look at him. "What's going on?"

He shrugged. "I don't really want to talk about work right

now." He brushed her hair back from her face. "We have only a few minutes. I want to get to know you again. Tell me something about you. Anything."

She scowled at him. "Well, for one thing, I get cranky when people blow me off."

He raised his brows and regarded her. "I feel like you just laid down a minefield that I'm supposed to walk through."

She thought about that. "I guess I did."

He paused. "The last time we made love, it took about five minutes for all the shit to rain down on us. Is that what is about to happen?"

"No." She felt a little defensive and folded her arms across her chest. "I just felt like you totally dismissed me when I mentioned the bakery."

"Ah..." He grimaced. "Well, that's because I did."

She let out her breath. "Keegan, that's not okay—"

"I'm sorry about that. The bakery's not going well, and I didn't want to bring that vibe into this moment." He took her hands. "Sofia, I haven't seen you in sixteen years. We just made incredible love. There's a decade and a half that time washed away between us." He pressed a kiss to her knuckles. "We have time to wade through the crap that we're both carrying. But a first date is supposed to be about magic and sparkles and giggles."

"This isn't a first date. I don't sleep with guys on a first date."

"You didn't sleep with me. You surrendered to the bond that's been holding us together for almost twenty years. And it's the first time this time around, and I want to do it right this time. I want you to feel honored, treasured, and safe."

Her heart got a little melty. "That was a good speech."

He laughed softly, and then gave a little tug of her hands, pulling her off balance so she tumbled onto his chest. She yelped in protest, but before she could get free, he'd flipped her under him and straddled her, trapping her hands lightly above her head. "Sofia Navarro, I want to romance the hell out of you. I want to dance under the Christmas lights, kiss you under the mistletoe, and get in a fantastic snowball fight with you and Gabby."

Her irritation faded. "I'm highly suspicious of being romanced nowadays," she reminded him.

"Ah...you did say that." His smile became thoughtful. "Then maybe it's time for you to learn how to trust again."

Her heart suddenly tightened. Trust? Not have to guard her heart anymore? "It sounds great in theory," she admitted, "but I honestly don't want to become that vulnerable again."

"I get that." He rolled off her and tucked her against him, so that his chest was against her back. "All right. I'll start."

She wiggled her butt against him, loving the feel of his body against hers. "Start what?"

"Confessions that will make it impossible for you to fear me."

"I want to fear you. It's healthy to keep my guard up." The fact she meant it was a little depressing, but girl power came at a cost sometimes, right?

"I'm a baker. There's nothing manly about that."

She started laughing. "You're very manly. Baking isn't going to change my mind about that."

"I have a little ceremony with my family on every July seventh, which was mom's birthday, to celebrate her. Her favorite dessert was chocolate cake. We used to try to invent a better chocolate cake at least once a week. So I create a new chocolate cake recipe every year for her."

Okay, so that was really sweet. "I'm sure she knows, and she's there with you."

"I know she is. I can feel her smiling at me, so happy that I'm surrounded by my family."

Sofia sighed, suddenly missing her mom.

Keegan's arms tightened around her. "What's the sigh for?"

"Your story made me miss my mom."

He rubbed her back. "I'm sorry. I know you were close."

"We were." She trailed her fingers over his forearm. "I'm so glad every day that she didn't have to see what I'd married."

"Screw that. She's looking down at you right now, damned proud of who you are and that great kid of ours. Our moms are probably toasting us with champagne right now, rolling their eyes at how long it took their kids to find each other again, celebrating the fact that a sixteen-year-old rebel got us straightened out."

Sofia laughed. "My mom definitely would think that." Her heart already felt lighter. "Okay, confess something else."

"All right." He paused for a moment. "Christmas is my most and least favorite holiday."

She smiled. "Okay, I'll bite. Why is it your most favorite?"

"All the baked goods, baby. It's a baker's heaven!"

She laughed. "I thought you were going to say because you get to celebrate with your family."

"That, too, but I don't want to give them all swelled heads. Gotta keep them in line, you know."

The warmth in his voice made her smile. She had to admit, she was a little jealous of his huge family, and having so many people at his Christmas dinner. "Why is it your least favorite?"

"The damned mistletoe."

"What did mistletoe ever do to you?"

"It hangs there, taunting me, mocking me because I have no one good to kiss. Every Christmas that goes by, I see that mistletoe and I think, 'damn, once again, I got no hot babe to make out with.'"

She laughed out loud then. "There's no chance that you

have a shortage of women to make out with. You're this hot celebrity billionaire."

"Exactly." He paused for a moment. "Sofia, you talk about how you have trust issues, but I have them too. After my mom died, I was tossed into a foster system that had nothing good to show me."

She rolled over to face him, tucking her hands against her chest while she listened.

"I learned I had to be on my own, and trust no one. Eventually, I trusted the Harts, and I still do. Completely. But when outsiders come knocking, they usually want something. None of us have formed deep friendships or bonds outside the family. Even Brody and Tatum knew each other from our under-the-bridge time." He looked at her. "It's a gift to be with you, to know that you want nothing from me."

She thought about that. "I do want something from you."

"Great." He tightened his arms around her. "I thought you'd never ask. How can I be your knight in shining armor?"

"Not mine. Gabby's." She paused. "Just don't break her heart."

He smiled. "That's it? That's all you want from me?"

"Yep."

"Promise." He leaned in. "What about her mom's heart?"

"Don't break that either," she whispered as his lips brushed over hers.

"Is it mine for the breaking?"

As he asked, they met gazes, and silence suddenly hung between them. God, she'd loved him with all her heart once. And then, she'd shut herself down. And now...temptation ran amok with this man who seemed to be put on this earth as the exact match to all the longings and needs in her heart.

"I'll go first."

She swallowed. "Another confession?"

"Always." He pressed a kiss to her knuckles. "That day you left after cutting out my heart with that speech—"

Oh, God. That speech. "I'm sorry—"

He kissed her to shut her up, before continuing. "When you left, I was shattered. Literally shattered. You'd given me hope again, and then, you were gone. My reaction was too extreme given that we'd had only a week together, but I was already broken by mom's death, and I put everything onto your shoulders to save me."

She bit her lip, listening.

"Now that I'm here with you, and I feel the difference in what is between us, I know that it was the only path. I had to find my strength on my own. And I did."

Her heart turned over at the truth in his voice. "We both needed to find our own ways," she agreed. "We were too young for anything permanent."

"Young, lost, and confused," he agreed. "But here's the thing. I'm none of those now. I know what I want. I know what's out there in this world. And I know that you're what I want. So, you might be keeping your heart to yourself, and that's completely fine, but mine is yours for the taking."

His words were so simple, so matter of fact, that she knew he was telling the truth. A part of her wanted to lean into him, to throw herself into this thing that felt so magical between them, but she couldn't. "That doesn't make sense. We literally have known each other for barely more than a week."

"Every forever-love starts with a first week."

God, he said the most perfect things. She wanted to throw herself into his arms...and run away at the same time. She felt her throat start to close up. "You sound like my ex. He said stuff like that. I believed him, but he was actually a monster."

"I'm not him—"

"I know that. But my instincts can't remember that." She pushed herself off the bed and grabbed her shirt. "Look, Keegan, maybe I'm just too broken for anything real."

"Sofia—"

She shook her head as she pulled her underwear on. "Please call me Sascha. It's the one thing that's only you. The way you say it wraps around me like a hug. I need you to be you. Only you." She held up her hand as he started to get up. "But not right now. I just need space."

Keegan leaned back in the bed, clasping his hands behind his head, watching her. His face was troubled. "Sascha," he said gently. "How can I help you?"

"Just give me space." She grabbed her shoes and socks and tucked them under her arm. "I'll see you later—"

"Will you? Or are you going to leave during the night?"

God, he looked beautiful lounging among the tousled sheets like that. "Last time we made love, it was in my hotel room. This time, another hotel room. What about a home? What about that?"

His brow furrowed. "You want to make love in a home?"

"No. Yes. I don't know. I need to go." She grabbed the door handle and pulled it open, but just as she walked out, she looked back over her shoulder. Keegan was sitting up in bed, the sheets draped over his waist, his forearms resting on his knees, watching her.

The look on his face made her heart stutter.

She felt like they'd just gone back in time, and she'd spat terrible things at him to try to wreck things badly enough to set her free, leaving him looking like "what the hell just happened?"

Was that what she was doing again? Trying to sabotage something wonderful just because she couldn't handle it?

Guilt shot through her, and she ran over to the bed. She

went down on her knees on the floor, and grabbed his arm. "Keegan," she whispered.

He looked over at her, and she could see the wall beginning to build between them. "What?"

"I—" God. She didn't even know what to say. "If I could pick any man in this entire world, past or present, to be Gabby's dad, it would be you." It was the biggest compliment she could think of, the grandest statement that she could give him to make him understand how worthy she found him.

He looked down at her hand on his arm. "And yet," he said softly, "you're going to go in there, get Gabby to pack her bags, and get a ride back to your car and be gone in the morning. Again. I can hear it in your voice."

"I—"

"What? Mom? Are we leaving?" Gabby appeared in the doorway. "And holy shit! You guys slept together?"

Sofia grimaced, and quickly stood up, while Keegan swore and yanked the comforter up over his lap. She quickly headed toward the door, leaving Keegan stuck in the bed, because he wasn't about to get up and parade around naked with Gabby there. "Gabby—"

"Mom." Gabby put her hands on her hips. "You are not going to make us leave, are you?"

"It's complicated—"

"It's not! You just make it complicated! God, Mom! He's nice! Bella's nice. Everyone's *nice*, and they want to be our family. Do you want another Christmas eve with two of us at the table? Another Christmas morning with the two of us? Don't you want anything more? Like, a huge family that is welcoming us with open arms?"

Sofia bit her lip. "Gabby—"

"Unless you don't want us?" Gabby spun toward Keegan. "Is that it? Is my mom trying to protect me from rejection? Do you not want me?"

"Fuck no." Keegan grabbed his jeans from the floor and shoved them under the covers, trying to get dressed. "You're my kid, Gabby. I'm all in. I want to get to know you. I want whatever role you'll have me in your life."

"And my mom? Do you hate her for not telling about me?" Tears filled Gabby's eyes. "Did you break her heart?"

Sofia's heart felt like it was going to snap in two. "Gabby, no. It's not him. It's me. I...I think I'm breaking his heart. Maybe. Again."

Gabby whirled toward her. "So, he wants both of us?"

Sofia glanced helplessly at Keegan as he threw back the covers and got out of bed, now wearing his jeans. "He—"

"I can speak for myself." Keegan walked over and went down on one knee in front of Gabby, so he was looking up at her. "Gabriella, what happens between your mom and me has no impact on you and me."

"That's not true, and we all know it."

"All right," he acknowledged. "Yes, it will have an impact, but it doesn't affect how I feel about you."

Gabby stared at him. "Did she leave you back then? Did she walk away from you? Is that why she won't tell me? Because she was in the wrong?"

Oh, God. "Gabriella, that's enough—"

Gabby spun toward her. "You're ruining it again, aren't you? He's my *dad*. You don't get to take him away from me again! You kept us apart, and it would have been so easy for you to let us become a family at any point, because clearly, he's totally fine with having me. But you didn't give us a chance. And now we *have* that chance again. He wants both of us, and you just want to wreck it again, don't you? Sleep with him, then walk away again? Well, forget it! I'm not going! You don't get to do that to me anymore!"

She whirled around, raced back into their bedroom, and

slammed the door shut, leaving Sofia and Keegan standing in his room.

"She's not wrong, you know." Sofia and Keegan both turned to see Bella down the hall, holding the puppy. "Didn't mean to eavesdrop, but I was bringing Millie back, and I heard the commotion."

"Bella," Keegan said, his voice low. "Stay out of this."

"No." Bella walked up. "Gabby's right. Keegan did deserve to know about her, and he would have been a great dad all along."

Keegan swore. "Bella, seriously—"

She waved him off and came to a stop in front of Sofia. "You were wrong to keep them apart."

Sofia fisted her hands, preparing for the accusations she knew she deserved.

"But it's okay," Bella said, taking Sofia off-guard. "We've found each other now, all of us, and we just go forward from here. It's also okay that you're struggling to trust him, to trust us," Bella said. "I get that. We all do. We all have trust issues. Keegan might have fallen head over heels for you again, but he'd never hurt you. My brother is one of the best guys on the entire planet, and you and Gabby are safe with him."

Tears clogged Sofia's throat at Bella's unconditional acceptance of her. "I don't know what to say—"

Keegan took her hand. "Bella, maybe go chat with Gabby for a moment. Help her not to be so mad at Sofia. We'll be right in."

Bella nodded. "Millie will help. Come on, sweetie." She knocked lightly on the door. "It's Millie and Bella," she called out. "Let us in."

The door opened immediately, as if Gabby had been listening at the door the whole time, which she probably had. Her eyes were red-rimmed, but she refused to look at Sofia as Bella and Millie slipped inside. The door closed behind them, and Sofia heard the deadbolt slide shut, making it impossible for her to get inside until Gabby was ready.

She held up her hands helplessly to Keegan. "I don't know what to do right now."

Sympathy flashed across his face, then his face became thoughtful. "You want to get out of here for a little bit?"

"I'm not having more sex."

He grinned. "No. Fully clothed. I have an idea."

"Gabby might need me—"

"I don't need you," Gabby shouted through the door. "I'm mad at you. Go away with Keegan."

"I'll stay with her." Bella cracked the door enough that Sofia could see Gabby sitting on the floor with Millie.

Her body language made it clear that her daughter was fuming. "Gabby—"

"Mom!" Gabby looked up, and to her relief, Sofia saw only anger on her face. No tears or fear or worry. Just anger. "Seriously. Go."

Anger she could live with. "All right. We'll be back...when?"

"A few hours," Keegan said. "Grab your warmest clothes and boots. We'll grab the rest from the truck."

Bella grinned. "There are hats and gloves in the truck. Whatever you need."

"Great. I'll just grab some stuff, but I promise not to make actual eye contact with you, Gabs."

"Good. Eye contact is illegal until further notice." Gabby appeared to be telling the new rule to the puppy, who was licking Gabby's face.

Sofia smiled to herself at Gabby's reply. She'd be okay. She could feel it in her daughter's voice. While Keegan waited in the hall, Sofia ran inside, grabbed her warmest socks and some more layers. By the time she got her boots on, she could see Gabby watching her out of the corner of her eye.

Ready to go, she crouched in front of her daughter. "Hey, babes. I love you."

Gabby didn't look up. "I love you, too," she muttered.

Sofia patted her daughter's shoulder, then stood up, surprised to see Keegan and Bella watching them. "What?"

"That's just really sweet," Bella said. "I forgot what a good mom is like."

Empathy flooded Sofia. She might have lost her own mom, but she had loved her like crazy. "I try," she said simply.

"That's enough," Bella said. "More than enough." She cleared her throat, then lifted her chin. "You guys go. Gabby and I have plans."

"Room service?" Gabby asked hopefully.

"Lots of it. And movies."

As Bella and Gabby settled on the bed to start going over the room service menu, Sofia stood up. She watched them for a moment, realizing how beautiful it was that Gabby had found this family. Family who loved her. How could she have gotten mad about that?

Keegan touched her lower back. "Ready?"

She startled, then turned toward him. "Yep. Where are we going?"

He grinned. "It's a surprise."

They began to head toward the door. "It's almost ten. What could there be to do?"

He grinned. "I'll use my money and celebrity to open doors."

"See, Mom?" Gabby shouted. "He's a keeper!"

"Not that you're superficial or anything," Sofia teased as she stepped outside.

"That would be impossible for me with you as my mother. Morals literally bleed from my pores every time I sweat."

Both she and Keegan burst out laughing at that remark, and she waved to Bella and Gabby as she shut the door. Her heart feeling lighter, she turned to Keegan. "All right. Bring it on, baker boy. Let's go make some donuts."

"Oh, we're definitely not making donuts." He gestured toward the elevator, and then, as she moved past him, he put his hand on her lower back.

It felt good.

So she let him keep it there.

CHAPTER TWENTY-ONE

Keegan was hooked.

On Sofia.

On Gabby.

On this second chance that he hadn't even known was possible, let alone something he actually wanted.

As he drove, he grinned as Sofia chatted animatedly, telling him about the time Gabby started reading the romance novels in her store, shouting out the sexy words to ask what they meant, and how Sofia invented meanings for them that were so silly and goofy.

He loved their mother-daughter relationship.

He loved that talking about Gabby lit Sofia up the way that he remembered her. The spark was still there, but at the same time, she was so shut down, that he'd almost lost her after they'd made love.

But she hadn't run, and now he had a chance to start building the trust.

He pulled off the main road and drove under a sign that said Blue Ridge Stables. He smiled when he saw the white Christmas lights strung up along their mile-long driveway. It had been a few years since he'd visited Blue Ridge Stables at Christmas, but it was even better than he remembered.

Anticipation built as he neared the turn in the driveway, waiting for Sofia's reaction. The moment he turned, she gasped. "That's incredible."

"Right?" The owners of Blue Ridge Stables decorated their house, barn, and stables with more Christmas lights than was probably legal. Thousands and thousands of twinkling lights lit up the night, wrapping around fences, trees, rooflines, horse vans, their front porch, and even their trucks. "Magical."

"Completely." Sofia was leaning forward, her hands on the dash as she drank in the festive atmosphere. "I've never seen anything like it. I feel like we're at the North Pole. All the ice on everything makes it look even more magical."

"It sure does." He remembered his first time: total awe.

Experiencing Sofia's reaction made him appreciate it even more. "I forgot about it until just now. We'll have to bring Gabby another time."

Sofia flashed him a grin. "She probably thinks she's too old for Christmas lights, but I love it."

"I thought you might." He parked by the barn. "They take donations in exchange for drive-throughs. Traffic can get congested here during normal hours, but they're closed now."

She raised her brows, her face glowing. "You bought us a private showing?"

He grinned. "Sure did. Plus, we've worked with Blue Ridge to rescue horses before, so we help each other out. I told Zach I had a girl to impress, and what guy is going to say no to that?"

She rolled her eyes, but she was smiling when she got out of the truck.

Energy raced through Keegan as he exited his vehicle and

jogged around the front to meet up with Sofia. The driveway had been sanded and the footing was fine. He took her hand, and gave a little internal fist pump when she didn't pull away. "This way." He led the way into the barn as the big double doors slid open, revealing a gorgeous, state-of-the-art stable absolutely filled with Christmas decorations. Sparkling light strands were everywhere, and a massive wreath at least fifteen feet in diameter hung up on the side of the hayloft. A Christmas tree was in the corner, and Keegan knew from experience that the presents beneath it were all for families in need.

He knew, because it was the Hart Youth Center that went around and collected the presents to distribute.

"Holy cow," Sofia whispered. "This is incredible."

"Yeah, it's a contest every year between their barns and ours, to see which has the most Christmas lights."

She looked back at him. "Seriously? Your barn looks like this?"

He nodded. "It has to. We host the Hart Youth Center Christmas Festival, and we have to do right by the kids."

Sofia smiled. "Of course you do." She squeezed his hand slightly, her face softening. "You Harts are good people."

"We try," he agreed, heartened by her willingness to see his family as not so scary. Progress was good.

At that moment, the owner, Zach Stephens, walked into the main area, leading two horses that were tacked up and ready for riding.

Keegan smiled when he saw his old friend. "Zach. Good to see you." He gave the cowboy a hearty handshake, then laughed when Zach dragged him in for a hug. They'd been through a few things in their time, and their bond was forever.

He'd wanted to bring Sofia here because the decorations were amazing, but also because Zach was a good man, and the vibe he gave off would help her relax. "Zach. I'd like you to meet Sofia."

"Sofia." Zach tipped his cowboy hat back and gave Sofia a big grin. "Any woman who gets Keegan's attention is a woman I want to know. That boy doesn't get around much when it comes to the ladies, so you must be pretty special."

Sofia smiled, her cheeks flushing with pleasure as she shook his hand. "Thanks. I don't hang around men much either, so we're a good fit, I guess."

At her words, Zach gave her a speculative look. "Whoever the guy was who convinced you that men suck was a bastard. We're not all like that."

Sofia's smile faded at Zach's perceptiveness, but she nodded. "I'm trying to remember that."

"Good. You picked the right guy to learn that from. If I had a sister, I'd be damn pleased if she picked Keegan, and I know just about every damn secret he has."

"All right," Keegan said, chuckling. "That's enough. She's going to think I bribed you and not believe a word you say."

Zach ignored him. "Sofia," he said, turning to her. "If Keegan's out here calling in favors to give you a special Christmas, then I take notice. He'd do it for homeless kids, or his mom-and-pop customers, or his family, but for a woman? Nope. So, welcome with all my heart."

A genuine smile filled her face. "Thank you," she said, glancing at Keegan.

"All right, let's get riding before you win her over with your silky words," Keegan gruffed. "Zach is the opposite of me with the ladies." At least that was the image Zach put on. Keegan knew there was a lot that Zach kept hidden, except from his closest friends.

Zach winked. "I'll never settle down. Too many women need loving, but yep, I got your horses."

Sofia raised her brows at Keegan. "A horse ride?"

"We've got the best Christmas trail ride in the country," Zach said. "We usually take folks out on the hayride, but friends get horses. Hop up."

Sofia's face lit up. "I haven't ridden in so long, but I love horses!" She gave Keegan a beaming smile. "Which one's mine?"

"You get Sally," he said, indicating the gray mare on his right. "I wasn't sure of your skill, but she's rock solid. She'll take care of you."

"Sally." Sofia walked up to Sally and stood in front of her. She ran her hand over Sally's dark, velvet nose. "I want you to know that I'll take care of you, too," she told the horse. "You're awesome, beautiful, and I appreciate you." Then she leaned in and gave the horse a kiss right on the nose.

Zach looked over at Keegan, a wide grin on his face "Anyone who's nice to Sally is on my good list."

Sofia laughed again, her voice so light and full of joy that Keegan and Zach grinned at each other. "Who do I have?" Keegan asked.

"This is Kingsman" Zach said. "We rescued him a couple weeks ago from a rough situation. Took him for a few rides and he seems okay, but I thought it would be great to get him out with an experienced rider and see how he does."

"Great." Keegan noticed then that Kingsman was a little thin, and the quarter sheet they had on him to keep him warm didn't hide the roughness of his coat. Like the Harts, Zach took in plenty of rescues, with many of them ending up at the Hart's sanctuary as permanent guests. He took a moment to rub Kingsman's nose, touching base with the horse, building the trust.

After a moment, Kingsman let out a deep sigh, then lowered his head, pressing it against Keegan's chest.

Zach nodded. "I thought you might be able to reach him. You always do. Still don't know why you give all your time to cakes instead of the horses. You're so damned good with them."

"Baking's in my heart."

"So are horses, or they wouldn't relate to you like that."

Keegan was aware of Sofia watching him, but he didn't look over. He didn't want to talk about baking. "Want a leg up, Sofia?"

She nodded, still watching him thoughtfully.

"All right." He walked over to her, clasped his hands around her bent left leg. "On three. One. Two. Three." He lifted at the same moment Sofia hopped, and she popped over Sally's back, landing easily in the saddle.

Kingsman was a little jittery, but after a few moments, Keegan was able to soothe him enough to mount him. Zach waved them off, and then Keegan led the way out the rear doors, soothing Kingsman as the gelding danced sideways, his feet clip-clopping on the wooden floor.

"You want an easier horse?" Zach called out, watching him. "So you don't need to focus on him?"

"No chance. We're good." He tipped his cowboy hat at Zach, then grinned at Sofia. "You first. Out that door."

She was still watching him thoughtfully. "All right." She urged Sally forward, and Keegan followed.

Her low gasp told him the moment she'd seen what he'd brought her there to see.

CHAPTER TWENTY-TWO

SOFIA HAD NEVER SEEN anything like it.

Stretching ahead of them was a mulched trail, winding through the woods, the entire thing lined with Christmas lights and strands of white globes, strung up along garlands of greenery. On every post was a Christmas wreath, and the trail stretched down the hill and through the woods, as if a fairy had left a trail of glittery pixie dust for them to follow into fairyland. "It's literally magical," she whispered.

She felt like a little girl again, swept up in the magic of Christmas. She wanted to run through the lights, dancing and twirling and singing, laughing like a two-year-old who had just discovered a miracle.

"I'm glad you like it. I stumbled across it, and I used to come here every year. My family would rent out the place, and it would be ours. I've been so busy with work that I forgot about it."

"How can you forget about this?"

"I don't know. Life happens, I guess. Now that I'm back, I can't imagine how I let this go by."

She looked over at Keegan, surprised by the edge to his

voice. There was something weighing him down so much. "Are you okay?"

He grinned. "You bet. Glad to be here. Ready to ride?"

This time, she didn't take his evasiveness personally. She knew about secrets. Who was she to ask him to trust her with his issues when she was having trust issues already? She understood. "Oh, yes. Do we just ride down the trail?"

"Yep. If you go fast, you can get through in an hour or so, but I've been known to be out here for a couple hours. You set the pace. I'll adjust."

"All right!" Her heart dancing with the magic of the holiday, she urged Sally into a jog. The mare's gait was like riding on a cloud, and she settled easily into the rhythm. The air felt bright and crisp in her lungs, and she loved the feeling of the breeze on her face.

Keegan rode beside her, chatting with his horse, and she felt the peace of his companionship. They weren't talking to each other, which gave her space to relax into the warmth and strength of his presence. His horse was antsy and skittish, and he kept shying, clearly nervous. Keegan had his hands full with his mount, but his body language was relaxed, and his constant crooning to the horse felt like a warm gift wrapping around her.

As they rode, she could see Kingsman's ears flicking back to listen to Keegan, as incapable as she was of resisting his voice.

The mulched, sanded path muffled their horse's hooves, making it almost feel like they were flying as they rode through the trees and under the light. There was a full moon, which allowed her to see into the woods they were passing. All was still, except for them, making her feel like they were all alone in the world, alone with the peace and spirit of Christmas.

Every so often, one of the light posts would host a small

Christmas tree, or a lighted candy cane, or a Santa. Periodically, the lights would crisscross across the trail, so they were riding below them. It was a winter wonderland that clearly took many loving hours to put up and maintain, created for the sake of giving Christmas spirit out into the world.

They'd been riding for about fifteen minutes, when she looked over at Keegan. He was leaning forward, talking to his horse, stroking his neck. Kingsman had settled down, his head lower now, his body relaxed. She could almost feel the horse's relief at being able to trust Keegan and his environment. It was how she'd felt in Keegan's arms, before she'd gotten scared again.

She slowed Sally to a walk, and Keegan gently reined in Kingsman, inviting the gelding to keep pace with her and Sally. "He trusts you," she said, watching the pair. "It's beautiful to see him relax."

Keegan grinned, his eyes dancing. "He's a great horse. You can feel his kindness beneath the fear. There's nothing like reaching past a horse's fear and helping them rebuild their confidence. It's an incredible feeling to have this majestic animal invite you into his inner circle."

His voice was reverent, and she smiled. "Do you work with horses on your ranch?"

He shrugged. "I used to, but I spend most of my time on bakery business now. It's growing quickly, and the business side is taking a lot of my time."

There was that edge to his voice again, and suddenly, she understood. "I remember when we were teenagers, you told me how you loved baking, because it felt like home, like your mom. It wasn't about the baking, so much as how it made you feel."

He glanced over at her. "You remember that?"

"Of course." She bit her lip, not sure whether to keep going or not. "Does the bakery make you feel like that?"

149

"Of course—" He cut himself off and was silent for a long moment. Finally, he looked over at her. "No. It doesn't. It feels like a business."

"Do you feel like your dream failed you?"

His gaze sharpened. "What do you mean?"

"Well, you opened the bakery because baking was your greatest joy. Because it was the home and love and security you lost. And now that you have the bakery, it doesn't feel like that. So, you worked so hard for so long to make it come true, and it didn't give you back what you wanted from it."

Keegan stared at her for so long that she began to shift uncomfortably in the saddle. "Sorry. I know you didn't want to talk about it before, but I wanted to help—"

"Son of a bitch," he muttered. "You're right. In fact, it actually steals me from my family and the horses. It keeps me from delivering the goods to the local businesses, like Alice. It takes me away from the things that give me the joy."

Her heart fluttered. She'd helped him? That felt so good. "So, this thing you spend all your time on, doesn't actually make you happy the way you thought it would?"

"*Fuck.*" He shook his head. "I've been trying to pin down what's wrong for months, and you nailed it. That's exactly it."

She grinned. "What are you going to do about it?"

He shrugged, but this time, it was thoughtful, not dismissive. "I don't know. I need to think about it." He grinned. "Thank you, though. It took you to put your finger on it, and I appreciate it."

A warm feeling filled her. "You're welcome. Thanks for letting me help."

He nodded. "Sorry for shutting you out. I didn't want to drag you down."

"That's what relationships are," she said. "The ups and downs."

He cocked an eyebrow. "Are we in a relationship, then?"

Her cheeks heated up. "Of sorts."

"Of sorts," he repeated softly. "I'll take that."

She grinned, appreciating the fact that he hadn't pushed further than that. He'd let her take the space she needed, which meant she didn't have to push him away. Relief rushed through her, and suddenly, she felt like his horse: able to relax into his attention without fear that something was going to scare her. She beamed at him, suddenly feeling light and free. "Want to race? And by race, I mean, a slow, relaxed lope?"

He laughed. "You bet. Let's do it." He urged his horse forward, and she did the same. She laughed with joy as they rode down the lightened trail, chatting and having fun, having easy conversation that wasn't about secret babies, ex-husbands, or mind-blowing sex. It was just friendship, and it felt amazing.

It made her realize that she wasn't simply attracted to him.

She liked him as a person. As a friend. And as a lover...

But as a forever? She dismissed the thought. It was more than she was ready for. More than she could handle.

She would just take this moment for what it was: the most magical, most romantic Christmas moment of her life.

CHAPTER TWENTY-THREE

BY THE TIME the threesome got back to Keegan's house Sunday afternoon after dropping Bella off at her home, Sofia was both tired and happy.

Bella and Keegan were truly good people, and their love for Gabby was heartwarming.

Bella was hilarious, and Sofia felt like they could be real friends.

And Keegan had kept things light and fun with her, keeping the pressure off.

She'd been able to relax...but at the same time, being with him made the pressure mount, because it gave her space to feel that connection that had always been there with them. The same electricity that had zapped them together last time was even stronger.

She wanted to be with him. She felt this deep calling to open herself to him, to let him in, to settle deep into the warmth of his soul and body, and find that magic place that the two of them created when they were together.

And that scared the living daylights out of her. It was too much, too fast...right?

Except that she wasn't desperate for a man. For a relationship. She was happy, independent, and fulfilled in her life. So, it wasn't as if she was falling for him because she didn't want to be alone, or couldn't be alone. Which meant, her response to him was...real? Right? Trustworthy?

The Hart family party was tonight, and she wasn't sure she wanted to be a part of it. But at the same time, she did. What if she didn't like them, and then things would get complicated with Keegan, especially if Gabby wanted to claim them as her family...or if she didn't.

But even worse...what if she fell madly in love with his family? What if being at that party made her heart start to yearn for the family that she didn't have? What if she fell as hard for his family as she had for him? Then what? Move to Oregon? Give up her life? Risk everything because now she was vulnerable?

She'd made stupid choices before when she cared too much. She couldn't be like that again.

"Welcome to my humble abode," Keegan said, interrupting her cascade into mental craziness.

"Holy crap," Gabby said. "That's incredible!"

Her daughter wasn't wrong. "I had no idea bachelors had this kind of taste," Sofia teased, trying to keep the tone light. But in truth? His house was gorgeous. If she could have designed a dream home, it would be the one that Keegan owned. It was a beautiful, rustic mansion that was somehow massive and homey at the same time. Rustic wood, huge glass windows, and a wrap-around porch. The yard was covered in icy snow, but it was expansive, with beautiful landscaping that was rustic and natural, and yet perfect. She could only imagine what it was like in the spring and summer.

He even had a covered gazebo on the south side of the property, beautiful white wood with incredible carpentry that made it look like an oasis. "Do you sit in the gazebo?"

He grinned, clearly hearing the deep longing and awe for a moment, even just one, out in the gazebo. "It's my favorite part of the house. I used to spend a lot of time out there watching the sunset before the bakery took off."

"I bet." Again with the bakery issue. His dream definitely had shadows. She understood that. Her dreams had become nightmares. "Maybe it's time to start watching sunsets again."

He slanted a look at her. "Sunset's in an hour. You up for it?"

She grinned. "Maybe."

"Oh, come on! You guys are going to go sit in the gazebo? What about the house?" Gabby leaned over the front seat as Keegan parked the truck. "I want a tour. Can we do that?"

"You bet."

"Sweet!" Gabby leapt out of the truck. "You really live here? Alone? It's crazy!"

Keegan chuckled. "Yep. You can pick any bedroom."

"Wait. Bedroom?" Sofia shook her head. "We need to get on the road after the party."

"What?" Gabby spun toward her, looking crushed. "But I want to stay. I want to meet their horses and see the barn."

"My Christmas party at the store is tomorrow evening. I need to get back." She was glad she had the party as an excuse, because Gabby was right. It *was* tempting to lose herself in this world...but that's what it would be: losing herself. She'd done that before: tempted by money, security, and heart-melting words.

It would almost be easier to trust herself if Keegan wasn't so attractive, rich, and charming, with a great sister. If he wasn't her daughter's biological father. All those factors were so damn amazing, so how could she trust that she just wanted *him?*

"Have Jocie run the party," Gabby said. "She's totally capable."

"She is," Sofia agreed, "But it's my store."

"Doesn't it get old to always be working at that store? If you married Keegan, you wouldn't have to run a store. You could just kick back and be waited on. Wouldn't that be awesome?"

But Sofia stiffened. "No. It wouldn't. Every woman should be financially independent. Otherwise, she can't make the choices she needs to make. Plus, I do it because it matters to me. I love the community I've nurtured at the store. They're our family, and I want to be there with them."

Gabby rolled her eyes. "You're such a nerd, Mom. They aren't family."

"Really? Because I'm pretty sure that all your babysitters came from there. And our Thanksgivings usually involve someone from the store. And Easter. And Dottie came to all your field hockey games. And—"

"Okay, okay." Gabby threw up her hands. "Fine. Whatever."

"Family isn't biological," Keegan offered. "Family is in the heart."

"Right?" Sofia's tension eased ever so slightly. Keegan got her, and she got Keegan. She met his gaze. "Family is in the heart."

He nodded. "There's a reason why we chose Hart as our family name."

She blinked. "Really? I never thought of that before."

"Absolutely. We had nothing, but we had each other. Eventually, I understood that meant we had everything." His gaze swung to Gabby, who was listening. "Or, I thought I had everything until I found out the spirited rebel who stole my heart years ago was still alive, and that we had a daughter. Then I realized that I hadn't had everything yet. But there was a chance for it."

Sofia and Gabby stared at him, both of them silent.

Gabby's eyes were wide with vulnerability, her mouth slightly open, as if she had no idea what to say or how to respond. Not sure whether to throw herself into his arms or to run away and protect herself.

Sofia realized in that minute that just as she was afraid to fully trust Keegan with her heart or Gabby's, her daughter felt the same way. Too much to hope for? Too good to be true? They'd both had to be so closed off for so long. How could they throw their hearts at him like that?

Suddenly, she knew they both needed space from Keegan. They needed room to find their footing again, and approach him from a position of strength. None of them had walked into this situation with any kind of preparation, and the emotions were hot and tangled.

"You know what?" Sofia said softly. "I think that it's getting late. We should head back to the store and skip the party."

Gabby's gaze shot to hers, and Sofia saw the conflict in her daughter's eyes. She wanted desperately to stay, but at the same time, she was scared, too. Afraid that if she fell hard, Keegan could break her heart.

Keegan frowned. "I'm not trying to pressure you," he said. "I'm just letting you know that I'm here for both of you. Always."

Gabby looked at Sofia, desperation in her eyes.

"Keegan," Sofia said. "Don't make promises you can't keep. Not to Gabby."

Keegan's eyes flicked to Gabby, and then he swore. "Hang on." He pulled out his phone and dialed.

A woman answered on the first call. "Keegan. Great to hear from you. What's going on?"

Sofia frowned. The voice seemed so familiar.

"Eliana? I have a woman here that you know. Her name is Sofia Navarro."

Eliana. Sofia's stomach did a somersault. Eliana was the attorney who had helped her disappear.

Eliana was quiet for a moment, then said, "No, sorry. I don't know anyone by that name. How's Dylan doing? I haven't heard from him in a while."

Sofia realized that Eliana was protecting her by immediately changing the subject. Eliana would never give up Sofia. Not even to a Hart. She'd always trusted Eliana, but hearing her protect her in person made her feel safer.

Keegan raised his brows. "Well, that's fine that you don't know her. I recently found out that I'm the biological father of her daughter, Gabriella. I want to create a trust fund for Gabriella. An irrevocable trust that gives her complete independence. How soon can you get that done?"

Gabby and Sofia looked at each other in shock.

Eliana was silent for a moment before she finally said, "Keegan, what are you talking about?"

"I need to get the money off the table. They need to not need me for anything. They won't trust me until they're free."

"Free of what?"

"Just free. Put the paperwork together. Create the trust. I don't need any information about them. Just send me the signature page and that's it."

Again, silence from Eliana. Damn. She was good. Sofia hadn't told even Eliana that truth. Eliana must be reeling in surprise, but she gave away nothing. Finally, Eliana said, "I'm sorry, Keegan, but I really don't know what you're talking about. I have no idea who this person is, and I don't do trusts anyway."

Women supporting women, even in the face of male, billionaire power. Eliana was tough, and that was the reason Sofia's ex had never been able to track Sofia through her. Damn. She wanted to be that tough.

At that moment, Sofia's cell phone dinged. She looked

down and saw a text from a person she had listed in her phone as Beyoncé...which was how she had Eliana's number stored. All Eliana had sent was a question mark.

That was their code. If Sofia ever needed help, all she needed to do was text a single character to Eliana, and Eliana would track her, find her, and do whatever it took to help her. An X. A question mark. The number 8. Any single character, and Eliana would unleash her hellhounds onto Sofia's tail.

She texted back. *Can I trust him with Gabby's heart?*

Eliana immediately answered Keegan on his phone. "My cat is coughing up a hairball. I need to deal with cat puke." She hung up, leaving Keegan staring at his phone.

"Cat puke?" he echoed.

Sofia put her arm around Gabby. "She's calling you back from her secure phone line. She always makes up funny excuses in case anyone is tapping her phone."

Keegan stared at her. "He's that dangerous?"

Before she had time to answer, his phone rang again. He answered it immediately on speaker phone. "Keegan here."

"What the hell is going on?" Eliana asked. "Sofia? Are you all right? Let me talk to her."

Sofia took Keegan's phone. "Hi." She hadn't spoken to Eliana in fifteen years, ever since they'd gone underground. "So, yeah, Keegan is Gabby's biological dad. It's complicated, but it's all out in the open now."

Gabby's cheeks turned red. "I'm sorry, Mom—"

Sofia put her arm around her daughter and hugged her. "It's all good, sweetie. But we're with Keegan now, and we're fine."

"He's a good man," Eliana said. "I've known him and his family for a very long time. You can trust him one hundred percent."

Sofia knew Eliana was answering the question she'd asked—

trust him with Gabby's heart. Keegan would stay by her daughter. Forever. No matter what. Relief filled her, and she suddenly felt overwhelmed. Eliana's sole professional focus was protecting women from men, usually husbands, boyfriends, and lovers. She would never, *ever* tell Sofia that Keegan was safe unless she was willing to stake her life on it. "Okay. Thanks." She meant it. She and Gabby exchanged glances, and she saw the relief on her daughter's face, relief reflected in her own heart.

She realized how badly she wanted to stop pushing Keegan away. To give him a chance. To give them a chance. With Eliana's backing, suddenly she felt like maybe she could at least keep the door open. See what happened.

Hope leapt through her. Did she really have a chance for the kind of love that she'd only dreamed of?

"Do you need anything?" Eliana asked her. "How are you and Gabby doing?"

"We're great. Happy. Well. Thank you for making it possible."

"I'm so glad to hear that, and of course, you are welcome." Eliana paused. "Are you out from hiding?"

"No. We just wanted to see Keegan."

"All right." Eliana paused. "Keegan, I love you, but your family is too public. Sofia, my recommendation is that you and Gabby stay away from all of them. It's too risky. One photograph online could be enough."

Sofia felt like Eliana had just reached out and yanked all the hope right out of her body, the fresh, new hope that she'd barely had time to process. "But if we're careful—"

"Paparazzi follow the Harts everywhere. Are you outside right now? If so, someone probably posted a picture of him talking to you."

Sofia thought of the video that had briefly streamed, and from the look of concern on Keegan's face, she knew he was remembering it as well. Gabby looked around and edged closer to Sofia.

"You've made it too far to make a risky choice now," Eliana said. "You need to get away from him as soon as you can. No offense, Keegan. If you want to stay in touch with each other, get some untraceable phones. But there's no way to stay invisible around him or his family."

Keegan swore under his breath. "Eliana, we can keep them safe. We're the Harts, remember? We have resources—"

"And make Gabby and Sofia dependent on your protection? They're free right now, Keegan. You'll never understand the gift that freedom is, until you've had it taken away. If you keep them, you will take away their freedom."

Sofia felt her heart closing down, and it hurt so much more now that it had been opened. *I can't go through this again.*

"What if we find him?" Keegan asked. "Make him a deal?" His tone made it clear what kind of a deal he would be offering.

"He's not the type of man you can threaten," Eliana said. "It would simply fire him up. The moment he found out Sofia was still alive and had a protector, he'd work ten times as hard to find her. For men like that, it's not about logic. It's about power and pride. Sofia, you and Gabby need to leave now. Go."

Gabby leaned into her, gripping Sofia's arm desperately. "Mom?"

Sofia looked desperately at Keegan, but even as she did, she knew it was stupid to look to him for help, not if it meant losing her freedom. Gabby's freedom. Their safety.

But they'd just found him. They'd just opened the door to possibilities that felt like a gift from the universe. Gabby's father. Sofia's first love...and second love...

"Hello?" Eliana said. "Are you guys still there?"

Sofia held her hands out helplessly to Keegan, and he

swore under his breath. "Yeah, we're here. It's not popular advice, Eliana."

"It's not my job to be popular. Sofia, are you leaving? Tell me you're leaving."

Sofia's gaze slid to the car she'd borrowed from Jocie, which, true to Keegan's word, had been moved to his house while they'd been delivering the Hart Bakery goodies. It was parked to the side, with chains already on its tires for the trip over the mountains to get back home. All she'd wanted was to get back to her store and to get space from Keegan, but now that it was being forced upon her, she didn't want to go.

She wanted to attend the Hart party with Gabby, to let her daughter meet her family. To experience a Christmas with the kind of family she'd always dreamed of having. A kiss under the mistletoe. A holiday of hope for love, for a family, for all the things she'd convinced herself she could live without.

All it had taken was Eliana snatching it away for Sofia to finally realize that was what she wanted.

But at what cost? Her life? Gabby's life? That cost was too high. The paparazzi too real. She would never ever forgive herself if she made the selfish decision to stay with Keegan and Gabby was endangered as a result.

It was Keegan who was strong enough to make the decision. "I'll have them leave," he said finally. "I'll hire security to see them home, just in case pictures have been leaked already."

"I'll have my team check as well," Eliana said. "Sofia, you know the drill."

The drill. The text that would come from Eliana or someone else, the one that meant run. Disappear. Forever. "I can't do that, Eliana. I can't disappear from my life. I love my life."

Gabby gasped. "Disappear? No!"

"I know," Eliana's voice softened. "We'll do whatever we can to keep you safe. But please, help yourself and go home for now. Keegan, do not approach him. At this time, as far as we know, he still believes she's dead. Don't open that door."

"Right. Okay." He hung up the phone, and the three of them stared at each other. "We can find him," he said quietly. "But it doesn't sound like that's a good idea."

Sofia shrugged. "For sixteen years, we've been hiding. I thought for a moment that we didn't need to hide anymore."

"Mom?" Gabby was holding her hand, something the teenager hadn't done for a long time. "What do we do?"

She took a breath. "We'll head home, and then figure things out."

Tears filled Gabby's eyes. "I don't want to go home. I just found them."

"I know. Me, too."

Keegan cleared his throat. "Both of you, into my house now. We'll wait in there until security shows up. No one's going to be taking pictures of you inside my house. But let's go."

Gabby spun around and ran for his house, but Sofia had a feeling it was more because that's where she wanted to be, not because she was scared to be outside.

Sofia glanced around the property as she followed Gabby, but she didn't see anyone. "Would there really be someone hiding in the bushes?"

Keegan put his hand on her lower back as they headed toward the house. "Not likely, no. But it has happened."

Gabby was already at the door, waiting for him to unlock it. He punched a code in the keypad, but the way he made Gabby put it in her phone so she would always be able to get in made Sofia's heart tighten. Such a strong statement of welcome went such a long way toward giving Gabby hope that Keegan meant it when he'd said he'd always be there for her.

They stepped inside, and both she and Gabby gasped. "This is gorgeous," Gabby blurted out.

"It really is," Sofia agreed. It was an oasis of warmth and home. Very casual, cozy, and comfortable, with big couches, a fireplace, and an open floor plan that let her see the gorgeous kitchen that was bigger than her entire apartment and store combined. Huge windows looked out onto nearby mountains and horse pastures, and there was even what looked like a covered pool in the backyard. The space was large enough for the entire Hart clan to gather with friends, but intimate enough that it would never feel lonely. "It's literally my dream house."

Keegan smiled as he hit a button on the wall that lowered the shades, hiding them from the view of the outside, and stealing their view. "Thanks. Make yourself at home while I make some calls. The kitchen's all yours. There's always some good food in there, between me and Bella."

"Awesome." Gabby headed straight for the kitchen, while Keegan took Sofia's hand and drew her toward the fireplace.

She went willingly, wanting to preserve every last moment with him before she had to leave. Keegan draped his arm around her shoulder, and she leaned against his side while he dialed. "Dylan," he said into the phone. "I need an escort for Sofia and Gabby. They need to head home ASAP. How soon can you get a couple folks here?"

While Keegan made plans, Sofia turned into Keegan, slid her arms around his waist and rested her cheek against his chest, while she watched Gabby going through the fridge. She noticed that there were Christmas lights strung up around the kitchen, a massive poinsettia on the island, and a huge, gorgeous Christmas tree in the corner of the living room.

The place was full of Christmas spirit, and it made her smile.

Keegan played with her hair while he made arrangements with Dylan, keeping them connected as he quickly explained the threat to Sofia and Gabby.

"What's his name? We'll go have a chat with him," Dylan said

Sofia smiled to herself while Keegan explained Eliana's concern, and Dylan argued. The Harts were all the same. Wanting to jump in and believing their power could stop anyone.

Maybe it could.

Maybe Eliana was underestimating them.

Or maybe Eliana had seen too many cases turn out wrong to be willing to take a chance, even the tiniest one.

After a few minutes, Keegan hung up. "Two escorts will be here in about two hours."

Two hours. They had two hours left.

He clasped his hands behind her lower back and rested his chin on her head while they watched Gabby. "Dylan's going to tell the rest of the family not to come over tonight. We'll reschedule."

"That makes me mad," Gabby announced. "One stupid asshat gets to control our lives? I'm so done with that."

"Me, too," Sofia said.

Gabby looked over at her in surprise. "You are? You're the one who's always telling us to stay low profile."

"I know. But being here has made me realize that there's a lot of life to be lived beyond our little life we created."

Gabby's eyes widened. "You want to move here and give up the store?"

Sofia laughed. "No, I'd never give up the store. But I don't want to live in fear anymore."

Gabby pulled out a loaf of pumpkin bread and set it on the counter. "So, what can we do?"

"I don't know."

"You guys can hide in my house for the next fifty years," Keegan said. "It's a nice house."

Sofia laughed at the hopeful look on Gabby's face. "No chance, babe."

"You're no fun." Gabby found a butter knife and cut herself a slice of the bread. "So, what do we do?"

"I still don't know." Sofia sighed as she leaned on Keegan's chest.

Gabby took a bite, then frowned. "This bread's not that good, Keegan."

He laughed, a low rumble that seemed to vibrate through Sofia. "I know. I've been working on the recipe for a while. I can't get it right."

"Apparently." Gabby pushed it aside and went back to the fridge. "What's it supposed to be?"

"Pumpkin bread." He paused. "You guys hungry? I can whip up something."

"If it's like the pumpkin bread, I'll pass," Gabby said, making Sofia laugh. She loved Gabby's comfort level with Keegan.

"I'm personally offended by that," Keegan announced. He kissed Sofia's head and then released her. "I'm making you food. I have to prove my awesomeness."

Gabby gave him a skeptical look, amusement dancing in her eyes. "My mom's a great cook. You'll never live up to what I'm used to."

Keegan shot Sofia a look. "Shall we team up? I'd love to see your brilliance in action. Maybe it'll inspire the solution to my pumpkin bread problem."

"I'll help, too," Gabby said. "I love cooking."

Sofia grinned. "It's a deal. Let's do it."

CHAPTER TWENTY-FOUR

As Keegan grabbed the wine out of the fridge a while later, he grinned as Gabby and Sofia burst into gales of laughter. He shut the door and as he headed back, he watched them descend into hysterics at his table, as they tried desperately to tell him the story of the time Sofia hid in the garbage can out front to scare Gabby when she got off the bus, only it didn't go as planned.

Their laughter filled his house with joy he hadn't known it was missing.

The sparkle in both their eyes was what he'd remembered from before, and it was infectious.

And the food had been amazing. And the pumpkin bread? They'd created a winner. The winner. The magic he hadn't been able to find on his own.

He'd loved cooking with both of them. It had felt like a family, not the Hart siblings, but *his* little family. They fit, this duo and him. He could feel it.

Sofia beamed at him as he approached. "That wine is amazing. You have to tell me where to get it."

"It's a local vineyard called Black Butte Vineyard. I can get you a case."

"I'll take it. Thank you." She was still laughing, her cheeks flushed, and her eyes sparkling.

"I'm going to check on the brownies," Gabby said, pushing back her chair. "You have to undercook them so they're chewy." She darted past him, grinning as she headed into the kitchen.

Keegan swung down in the chair beside Sofia. He rested his arm on the back of the chair, then leaned in to kiss her.

Her smile widened, and she leaned forward, meeting him halfway. The kiss was G-rated for Gabby's sake, but that almost made it more special, because it felt like a casual kiss that was simply part of their lives. Sofia put her hand on his chest, slowing down the moment as they kissed.

Gabby was oblivious, still chatting about brownies, and when Sofia pulled back, her gaze was dancing with amusement as she locked gazes with Keegan. He kissed the tip of her nose, and leaned in, lowering his voice. "This has been an amazing evening."

Sofia's smile widened. "It has," she agreed. "It's the first time we've been in a regular house together. It works, doesn't it?"

"It does." Hell, yeah, it did. "You know, if you stay here tonight, no one will know. It would be safe."

Temptation and longing filled her gaze, igniting an answering longing deep inside him. "I have the party tomorrow at the store. Our Christmas party."

"What time?"

"Six in the evening, but there's a lot to do. Food, decorations, name tags, organizing the gift bags." She smiled. "Everyone loves it. It's really a special group of women."

The warmth in her voice touched Keegan. He could tell

she'd created a real community in her store. Unlike him, when she'd turned her passion into a business, she'd successfully infused it with the sense of purpose and meaning that had been missing from his. "What if you got there early? Like at six in the morning?"

She shook her head. "If I drive through the night, I'll be dead tired in the morning."

He hesitated, not sure whether he was pushing it too far or not. "What about the jet?"

"The jet?" Gabby slammed the oven closed. "*The jet?* You're offering us a ride back home in your private *jet?*"

He grinned. "Yeah. We can take the smaller one, which can land at a regional airport near you."

"You have more than one? Holy cow, Mom! Let's do that!"

Sofia sat back. "We can't fly home in a private jet. The Hart jet? People notice who gets out of the Hart jet, don't they? And who gets on?"

"We can handle it. We'll take a car right up to the plane, then shield you when you get on. It'll be impossible for anyone to identify you. We can do the same on the other end. Obviously, it's not a sustainable long-term solution, but it works. Personally, I like it better than sending you on a six-hour drive through the icy woods alone. By the time you'd leave tonight, it'll be almost eight anyway. Catch some sleep, and we'll head out in the morning."

"That makes so much more sense," Gabby said. "We don't need to total two cars in two days, right?"

"I can have someone drive the car back," Keegan said. "It'll be dropped off at your house."

Sofia raised her brows. "It's tempting."

He grinned. "Good. All the guest bedrooms are made up. You can pick whichever one you want."

"I get first dibs," Gabby said. "Can I go look?"

He laughed. "Sure, go ahead."

"Awesome. The brownies are coming out in two minutes. Don't let them stay in too long! I'll be right back!" Gabby took off, her feet thudding up the stairs as she shrieked with delight.

Sofia laughed. "You're trouble, Keegan. You know that right?"

He pulled her in for a kiss. "Isn't that why you fell for me the first time?"

"I fell for you because you were you."

"All the better." He kissed her again, but this time, it was the deep, passionate kiss full of promise and temptation that he'd been wanting to do all day. He kissed her until they were both breathless, and when he pulled back, it was just enough to let them breathe, not enough to put any distance between them. "What do you say, Sofia? You want a sleepover tonight?"

She met his gaze. "Yes," she whispered.

Sudden joy pulsed through him. "I'll make some calls."

"Okay."

"I found the room I want," Gabby shouted. "Mom! Come look!"

Sofia stood up. "I'll be right back. Get those brownies out, or you'll break her heart. No teenage girl can handle overcooked brownies."

"I got it handled." He stood up, kissed her again, and then watched her jog across the floor in her socks, calling to her daughter. To *their* daughter.

Damn, it felt so right to have them there with him. Every moment was better than the last.

The oven timer went off, and he headed toward the brownies as he pulled out his phone again, to make new arrangements. Arrangements that were much more to his liking, because they gave him time with Gabby and Sofia, it enabled him to set more things in motion to keep them safe, and it gave him one night where he didn't have to worry about their safety.

Tonight, they were safe. Truly safe.

And he liked that. A lot.

CHAPTER TWENTY-FIVE

It was after midnight by the time they all went to bed, but Sofia couldn't sleep.

She lay on her side in the most beautiful bedroom she'd ever been in, watching the stars and moon light up acres and acres of the Hart Ranch. There were two big barns, and she wanted to go see the horses in them. The Harts owned a sanctuary for horses. A place filled with second chances, fresh starts, and unconditional love.

If she were a horse, she'd move in and stay forever and surrender to the beauty and healing of this place.

Instead, she would be getting on a plane in a few hours, leaving it behind before she even had a chance to explore it, returning to the home she'd created and loved.

Could she love two places? Could she belong to two places at once?

Not that she could come back here, according to Eliana.

Because the shadow of her past life still haunted her. But laying there, she felt so happy. Gabby was happy. And the secret that had been weighing her down for so long was finally free—

There was a light knock at the door, and she rolled over as Keegan slipped inside. He was wearing sweatpants, and that was it. He was muscled and strong, literally the sexiest man she'd ever seen in real life. He closed the door, then leaned back against it. "I know Gabby's down the hall, but I just wanted to check in and see how you were."

She tucked the pillow under her head. "You know, if I met you today, I'd be so intimidated by you."

He looked surprised. "Really?"

"Yeah. You occupy this huge space energetically. Money. Fame. Attractive as hell. Charming."

A slow smile curved his mouth. "Attractive?"

"You know you are, but that's not my point." She patted the bed, inviting him to come sit.

Keegan locked the door behind him, then walked across the floor, his bare feet silent on the thick carpet. He sat down on the bed and faced her. Not tackling her for lovemaking. Just there to connect, respecting that she might not want to do anything with Gabby a few doors down, because a home didn't offer the same privacy as a hotel room. "What's your point, then?"

She held out her hand, and he took it, entwining his fingers with hers. "My point is that to the world, you're this icon. Unapproachable. And you became that way to me when I started seeing you in magazines. You stopped being that boy I ran around with, and became this untouchable marble statue."

He rubbed his thumb over the underside of her wrist, a casual touch that connected them. "A marble statue? That doesn't sound great."

She smiled. "But the moment you walked into that tavern, you were simply Keegan again. The boy who saved me from a truck. A teenager who had lost his mom and lived under a bridge, who had nothing but his heart and his courage to offer."

He smiled. "I like how you phrased that. You make it sound like I had value back then."

"To me, you did. And you still do." She put her hand on his hip, needing to touch him. "I've been holding this secret about us, about who Gabby's biological dad is, for so long. It's been this constant weight in my heart, a fear of what would happen if she ever found out. A worry that one day, I wouldn't be able to keep the secret. Fear, a deep, terrifying fear, that my little baby would break if she found out the truth."

He said nothing.

"Keegan?"

He finally looked up at her. "Would you ever have told me?"

She hated to admit it, but she had to. "No."

"So, I would have died, never knowing I had a kid who was growing up without a dad? With a black hole in her life, a hole that I would have given all my money to be given the chance to fill? You would have let that happen?"

Oh, God. This was it. The conversation she'd been dreading. "Yes," she said honestly. "I didn't know that you would welcome her. I didn't know if you were a good man."

"How do you know if you don't give it a chance?"

She shrugged. "You're right. I was too afraid to try, but that's not an excuse. What happened with my ex was a long time ago, and there was no excuse to stay hiding in his shadow for so long." She let go of his hip. "I see that now, but without Gabby, I never would have dared to try."

"Do you regret your decision? To not tell me?"

She flopped back on the bed and crossed her forearms over her forehead. "Regret is deadly," she said softly. "It eats away at your soul until you have nothing left, and yet there is no way to ever change what happened in the past. So regret is simply a way to destroy yourself. I had a kid who needed me to shine for her."

"So, no regret?"

She looked over at him. "I can't afford regrets, Keegan. What I can do is learn from each moment and do my best with each day that I have." Would he understand that? It had taken her so long to learn how to live with herself, to learn to love herself, to learn to live with the choices she felt she had to make.

Keegan was quiet for a long moment, but he was continuing to play with her fingers.

She waited for his next question. Or his statement that she was a cold, heartless bitch. Or whatever was coming.

But instead, he stretched out beside her on the bed, clasped his hands over his head, and crossed his ankles. His body was pressed up beside hers, not in a sexy way, but in a companionship, a bond, a *forgiveness*.

Tears suddenly filled her eyes. "Keegan? Talk to me."

He rolled onto his side, and she did the same, so they were facing each other, their heads on the pillow. He traced his finger down the side of her face. "You're even more beautiful than you were back then." He wiped away a tear from her cheek. "Why the tears, sweetheart?"

"Because I just told you I don't regret not telling you about Gabby. It's a rough thing for someone to hear. It doesn't feel good to say that to you, but I have to be honest, because I wasn't honest before."

He smiled, his face warm, his mouth so close to hers. "Sweetheart, life is incredibly complicated. The choices we make are complex, and in the moment, each moment, we do the best we can. I know that."

"What have you ever done that you regret?"

He didn't hesitate. "I let the love of my life walk out of the door, and I didn't try to get her back."

Her heart turned over. "The love of your life?"

"Yes." He smiled. "And before you ask another silly question, I'll say yes, I'm referring to you."

Emotions clung to her like a sticky spiderweb, tangling her up. "Keegan—"

"That night, after we made love, and then you lost your shit at me, I let you go."

She stared at him. "Because I was horrible to you."

He laughed. "Sofia, I had been in foster care for two years. I could tell the difference between someone who was bad news, and someone who was striking out because they were scared. You were scared. I could see it in your eyes. I knew about being scared, because I was scared, too. Hell, every Hart was scared back then, too. I was only eighteen, but I'd seen more than I wanted to. So, yeah, I knew you were scared to death, and I let you walk out."

She frowned. "Why?"

"Because I was even more scared than you were."

"Of what?"

"Of losing someone I loved again," he said softly. "Losing my mom almost broke me. I had completely shut down. I had no intention of ever letting myself hurt like that again. But I fell in love with you, Sofia. I fell hard and fast for you, on every level. When I was holding you in my arms after we made love, I realized I was completely in love with you. All in. And that terrified me."

Her heart ached for the teenage boy he'd been. "And then I was mean to you."

He laughed softly. "No, babe, you set me free. You gave me the excuse to let you go, so I did, and I ran like hell back to my little hideaway under the bridge. You think you were hiding? That was me back then. Hiding for all I was worth."

She couldn't help the tear that slipped free. "Keegan—"

He put his fingers on her lips. "I started looking for you about two years later. Over the years, I hired private detectives, but no one could find you, because you'd apparently given me a fake name. I wanted another chance with you. I wanted a chance to find out what we could be."

She was wordless.

"A few days ago, Brody came to find me. He told me that they'd found you, and that you and your baby girl died in a car accident. I did the math, and realized that Gabby might have been my daughter. I felt loss that day, stunning tragic loss."

"Oh, God. Keegan. I'm so sorry—"

He took her hand as she was reaching for his face, and pressed a kiss to her fingertips. "And then a few hours later, a sassy teenager who looked like my childhood love, grinned at me, and said 'Merry Christmas, Dad. I'm home.'"

Sofia started laughing. "That's how she did it?"

"Yep, and then, when I realized you were on your way to get her, and not remotely dead, I knew that I'd gotten the second chance that no one ever gets. Going from thinking you were dead, and then having you on your way to my house made me realize that I wasn't going to mess it up this time, not if the connection was still there...which it is."

"It is," she whispered. "Definitely."

He let out his breath, as if he'd been holding it, waiting for her confirmation. "Sofia, I know you're scared and we're dealing with a lot right now, but I'm not letting you walk out that door, without making sure that you know that I love you. Completely. Unconditionally. Forever. You are loved. Loved. Loved. Loved. The kind of love that you don't need to fear. You have it from me. Always have. Always will."

The tears came for real this time. "Oh, Keegan," she whispered.

"And don't tell me that I don't know you. I do." He put

his hand over her heart. "I know what's in here, and I'm willing to take it as slow as you want to build things together, but you need to know that you're loved. I love you."

She could feel his love. Pure. Kind. Accepting. It was a good love, coming from a good heart, and a good man. *I love you, too, Keegan.* The words whispered through her mind, but she couldn't bring herself to say them. It was too soon. Too scary. Making a promise she didn't know if she could keep.

So, instead, Sofia scooted forward, framed his face, and kissed him. She poured her love into the kiss, her acceptance of his love for both her and Gabby, her total surrender to this incredible man.

The way he kissed her back, so thoroughly, so without hesitation, with so much tenderness made her want to kiss him forever.

She wrapped her arms around his neck and pulled him against her. He slung his leg over her hip and tunneled his hand through her hair, until they were completely entwined, igniting the night with the heat between them. The kiss became hotter and hotter, until she felt like she was burning for him, for them, for more.

She tugged at his pants. "Take these off."

He paused, his lips brushing against hers. "What about Gabby?"

She laughed and covered his lips. "Shh!"

He grinned, and then took over the kiss, rolling her onto her back as he moved over her. She knew then that he'd been holding back because of Gabby, but now that she'd given him the green light, he was going to pour it all on.

And it was delicious.

He palmed her belly, then slid his hand up her ribs and across her breasts, taking her tank top with it. He slid the straps over her arms, kissing his way along her collarbones.

Earlier, at the hotel, it had been hot and desperate, the culmination of a decade and a half of wanting.

This time, she felt the leisure in Keegan's kiss, as if he wanted to melt every moment into a timeless wonder of adoration, love, and ecstasy.

And she let him. Sofia surrendered completely to him, tipping her head back when he nibbled on her neck, as his hands found the waist of her shorts and tugged them over her legs, his hands gliding over her skin with seduction unleashed.

He stripped out of his sweats, and when he pulled her against him, there was absolute surreal joy of the skin-to-skin contact along the length of their bodies. Total surrender. Complete trust. Magical intimacy.

Keegan took his time with her, kissing and loving on every part of her body, one at a time, then back again, until her body and soul were a swirling inferno calling to him. To Keegan. No one else, but Keegan.

As he moved over her, she locked her feet behind his lower back, feeling his muscles flex beneath her touch. Her hands on his shoulders, basking in the strength that he'd surrendered to her.

Her body welcomed him, as if she had been waiting for him her whole life. The connection was brilliant, magical, and without any walls between them. He smiled at her. "My beautiful Sofia," he whispered as he leaned down to kiss her.

"Yours?"

"In my heart, yes. But free? Always." He moved then, distracting her before she could respond.

She went with it, surfing the waves crashing down around them, bigger and faster and harder, until she finally let go completely and let the wave take her, cresting with Keegan as they both gave in at the same moment, together, bonded, complete.

And shortly thereafter, she let herself fall asleep in his

arms, completely surrendering to him to keep her safe while she slept.

And in the morning, when she woke up, he was still there. Holding her. Entwined around her.

She smiled as she breathed in the feel of his body wrapped around her, realizing that she didn't feel trapped or panicked.

She felt happy. At peace. Like she was where she belonged. "Oh, Lordy," she whispered to herself. "This is much too complicated."

"Yep," Keegan said, surprising her, because she thought he'd been asleep.

She rolled over to face him, smiling when he kissed her. "Good morning."

"Good morning, my love. You ready for a trip on a private jet?"

She laughed softly. "A private jet isn't my thing."

"Well, lucky for you, it's my thing, so I've got you covered there. Teamwork makes the dreamwork, right?"

She rested her hand on his cheek. "It's so tempting to lie here forever."

"Right? We could get Gabby to wait on us. I'd bet she'd make a good minion."

Sofia laughed out loud at that. "What sixteen-year-old wouldn't make a good minion? They're all so malleable at this age."

"That's what I hear. I'm looking forward to finding out."

Her chest tightened slightly. "What kind of role do you want in her life?"

He smiled. "Sweetheart, I'll never get between the two of you. I couldn't even if I tried, because the bond you two have is incredible. I promise you that. I also promise you that she'll never have to wonder if she's enough for me. I'll never let her down, and I'll never hold her back. Other than that, how about we see how things unfold?"

Sofia nodded, her throat suddenly tight. "I wish my dad had been like that."

"Wish mine had too, but we can only move forward." He kissed her again, then smacked her lightly on the ass. "Let's get moving. Planes don't wait for anyone."

She propped herself up on her elbows as he got out of bed, totally checking out his sculpted rear end. "Won't your jet wait for you? Since you own it."

"Totally. I was just trying to be witty and hilarious. But your Christmas party won't wait, so off we go." He yanked on his sweats. "Meet you downstairs in fifteen?"

"You got it."

He dove onto the bed for one more kiss, and left her laughing as he jogged out the door and down the hall.

She lay back in bed and clasped her hands above her head. "What am I going to do about him?" she whispered.

Then Gabby came bounding in, and Sofia didn't have time to think about herself anymore.

Which was probably for the best.

CHAPTER TWENTY-SIX

"I MISS HIM, MOM."

Sofia looked over at Gabby, who had been serving up punch to their guests at the holiday party. "I know. Me, too." Their Christmas party at the store had been amazing. Seventy-five attendees, the most ever. Over a hundred gifts sat under the tree for the women's shelter. The trade-a-book table had been busy all night, with friends recommending books to new friends, and book addicts finding new treasures.

And she'd rung up a lot of money in sales as well, because what romance addict could go to a party in a bookstore and not buy more books?

But best of all was the laughter, the warmth, and the camaraderie of women at the party. Only two guys, both of them husbands who had fallen in love with the romance genre after deciding to see what their wives were spending so much time reading.

It felt like home, like Christmas, like where she belonged.

Which made everything so much more complicated, because Sofia also felt like she belonged in Keegan's arms at his home in Oregon.

Six hours was too far to commute to work on a daily basis, and it wasn't simply work. It was her passion.

Gabby sighed. "We can't even talk about him, because people care too much about what he does."

"I know." They hadn't even had the chance to talk much to Jocie, because as soon as they'd arrived, they'd been in full gear with party prep, with assorted volunteers and delivery people around all the time. Plus, honestly, she hadn't been ready to talk about it yet.

To Jocie, Keegan was a celebrity.

To her, Keegan was her heart. Not that she'd told him yet. She felt like taking that step was making promises she wasn't ready to make. Like, did that mean she needed to take her focus off her business to nurture the relationship? He couldn't move—his family was all in Oregon. But she didn't want to lose what she had either. And what if it didn't work out? Right now, they were cool together, but if things went terribly, how would that impact Gabby?

Saying good-bye to him on the plane had been hard. He'd remained inside to stay out of camera range, and his security team had hurried her and Gabby off the plane into an Escalade. It had been cool, actually. She'd felt like a celebrity, and it had been pretty crazy.

She looked out the window and saw the Escalade parked across the street. True to his word, Keegan had sent security. The men had been wandering around outside, keeping an eye out for any sign that her ex had found them.

How long would they stay?

How long until she didn't have to worry anymore?

The room was full and crowded, and everyone was chatting. It was perfect...but right now, it didn't fill her up the way it always did. It just felt...like it was missing something.

"Excuse me," a man called out from the front door.

Sofia and Gabby spun around, certain that it was Keegan,

but it was an older man in the door wearing a cowboy hat. He was hunched over, with a huge nose, and a paunch. He had enough wrinkles on his face to qualify as an old-west cowboy, and his jeans were old and tattered as well. He tipped his hat to the room. "Howdy, folks. I have the rest of the Hart's bakery order. Sorry we're late. Shall I set it up?"

Jocie stood up from her spot on the couch. "We have our complete order from the Harts. You must have the wrong address."

"Is this...hang on..." he shuffled around in his jacket and pulled out a receipt. "Thirty-six Main Street?"

"Yes, but—"

"Then I got stuff for ya."

At that moment, Sofia saw a little dog peeking out of the man's jacket.

"Mom?" Gabby elbowed her. "That looks like Millie."

"It does." Fear suddenly gripped her. Had something happened to Keegan?

The old cowboy shuffled over to Gabby. "Wondering if you could hold my little dog for me?"

He winked at them, and there was no mistaking the radiant blue of Keegan's eyes. Gabby's eyes widened. "Is that makeup?" she whispered.

"Best in Hollywood," Keegan whispered back. "Didn't want to miss the party."

Holy cow. He'd literally hired a makeup artist to disguise him so he could attend her party? That might be the sweetest thing she'd ever heard.

Within moments, Keegan-the-old-man had the roomful of ladies swooning to help him bring in the Hart's bakery items. His warmth and humor injected so much spirit into the gathering that had already been going so well. No one suspected the old man was actually a strapping, handsome, cowboy in his thirties.

Not only did he fit in her little world, but he added his charisma and warmth to make it even better. He took care of the hearts of her people, and that was so special.

He tipped his hat. "Well, ladies, that's the lot of it. I'll be on my way. Merry Christmas to all."

"Wait!" Sofia held up her hand. "Is this your last delivery of the evening? Would you like to join us?"

He cocked a bushy, gray eyebrow at her. "That's mighty nice of you, but this ain't my party—"

"Oh, stay!"

"We'd love to have you!"

Gabby grinned at Sofia while the crowd of romance-reading women left the cranky old delivery guy no choice.

"All right, all right." He held up his hands in defeat. "I can't disappoint a roomful of ladies, can I?"

The room erupted in cheers, and one of the Wednesday night book club's original members, a sassy senior named Pippy, grabbed his arm. "Come sit with me. We're going to read our favorite Christmas sex scenes. You can read the man's part when it's my turn."

Sofia started laughing when Keegan shot her a look of mock horror, but everyone thought that was such a great idea that Keegan wound up reading all the male dialogue for everyone's favorite scenes over the course of the evening.

It was hilarious listening to Keegan read the love scenes, and the attendees started picking more and more raunchy ones to try to get him to falter.

It was one of the best Christmas parties she'd ever hosted. So much love, warmth, and joy, which was everything that Christmas was about for her.

Keegan was adorably charming with all the ladies, but he never once crossed that line to flirting, even though, as an old man, he could have gotten away with a lot. But he didn't. He never made Sofia feel insecure, always shooting her private smiles, and finding ways to include her in the moment.

Even in the crowd of wonderful, fun women, he made her feel special, and he'd done the same with Gabby.

He was a treasure.

Jocie walked up and slung her arm around Sofia's shoulder. "We need to invite Kevin back for every party. He lights up the room."

Sofia smiled. "He is nice, isn't he?"

"He's a catalyst of joy, like someone else I know."

"Who?"

Jocie elbowed her. "You, you dingbat. The way he is, is the way you are. You bring out the best in people, even if you're not feeling at your best, you still have this way of lighting up those around you. Like Kevin does. You two would be a great match."

Sofia looked sharply at Jocie, wondering if Jocie had figured out who Kevin really was. "He's too old for me."

"And you're head over heels for Keegan anyway."

Sofia felt her cheeks heat up. "I didn't say—"

"You didn't have to," Jocie said. "You and Gabby have been glowing since you got back. I know you don't want to talk about it yet, and that's totally fine, but you can't hide it. You're so happy that you even look at Kevin like he's the greatest thing the world has ever created."

"I look at Kevin like that?"

"Yep. You look at him with all sorts of sparkly love in your eyes, which wasn't there before your little trip to Oregon."

Sofia sighed. "Dammit."

Jocie raised her brows. "That's bad news?"

"Oh, Jocie, it's so complicated. And Eliana said I needed to stay away from him, because paparazzi and fans love to take pictures of him, and I could get caught up in any of those photos."

"Oh..." Jocie frowned. "I guess that's true. But if you love him, isn't it worth fighting for? You walked out on him last time, so you're going to do it again?"

"I'm not walking out on him—"

"Mom!" Gabby hurried up. "Keegan said he'd take me for ice cream after the party. That's okay, right?"

"Keegan?" Jocie glanced at Gabby, then at Kevin, then at Sofia. "Holy crap! That's—"

Gabby grimaced, and Sofia slapped her hand over Jocie's mouth. "Ssh!"

Jocie nodded and pushed Sofia's hand away. "Holy crap, though! He got that makeup on so he could be at your party without anyone knowing it was him?"

"I'm sorry, Mom," Gabby said. "I wasn't thinking—"

"No, it's okay." Sofia was relieved actually. It was so difficult keeping secrets from her best friend. "We can trust Jocie." Jocie had been through hell and back with her ex, and she knew about dangerous men.

"Totally," Jocie agreed, watching Keegan with new interest. "No wonder you look at him like you're in love with him! And no wonder he's so happy. You guys are all so adorable together. Yay!"

Gabby grinned. "He's awesome."

"I can see that." Jocie beamed at Gabby. "I'm so happy for you, baby. And I'm so proud of you for stealing your mom's car to go after him. Sometimes a girl just can't listen to her mom."

"Jocie," Sofia said, trying not to laugh. "Seriously? She totaled my car."

"For a great reason! You definitely weren't going to take action, and see what you would have missed." Jocie pulled Gabby into a big hug. "Anytime you want to disobey your mom, you go right ahead and do it. You have great instincts."

"Thanks, Jocie." Gabby hugged her back, and stuck her tongue out at Sofia, which made her burst into laughter.

"Gabby," Keegan called out. "Want to help me bring more coffee cake in from the kitchen?"

"Yes!" She beamed at Sofia and Jocie, then took off, jogging over to Keegan as he waited for her. He nodded at Sofia, then followed Gabby into the kitchen.

Jocie sighed. "That might be the sweetest thing I've ever seen. He's literally wearing about fifty pounds of makeup and prosthetic so he can be with you tonight."

Sofia bit her lip. "But how does this work long-term? He can't wear makeup all the time."

"Find your ex and have him killed."

Sofia blinked. "You actually sounded completely serious there. That was a little terrifying."

Jocie grinned. "I didn't mean that, but it's tempting, isn't it?"

"Maybe a little," Sofia agreed. "But seriously. I don't know how anything can work. I'm not going to move down there, and he's not going to move up here, and how would we work it anyway? Besides, how do I even know he's as good a guy as he seems? I barely know him—"

Jocie hit her with a Christmas dishtowel. "Sometimes you talk too much. Stop trying to talk yourself out of something great. If he turns out not to be your true love, at least you tried. And if he does, well, then you'll owe your kid for the rest of your life for stealing your car."

"I'm not moving there. I can't give up my independence."

"No, but you can meet halfway. You can figure out a new way for your life to look, one that's even better than before."

"I guess, but—"

"Sofia." Jocie caught her arm. "Listen to me."

Sofia bit her lip. "What?"

"You were terribly scarred by a bad man. I know what

that's like, and I know it sits in your heart forever, and makes you not want to try again. I know that. You know I know that, right?"

Sofia nodded, emotions clogging her throat.

"But sometimes, despite our best efforts to stay alone, the universe gives us a gift. A person we can trust. We found that with each other, right? Friends til the end of time."

"Til the end of time," Sofia agreed.

"And what if Keegan's the same? Someone who will love you and have your back until the end of time? Are you going to hide from it? Make up reasons not to try?"

"I feel like that's not a bad plan—"

"It's a terrible plan. You're a smart, badass chick now. You don't need to hide anymore. He seems wonderful, and the vibe between the three of you is magical. Don't run and hide, Sofia. Live life. Trust your heart."

"It was wrong before," she whispered. "And I almost died for it."

"I know, baby," Jocie said gently. "But you're not that person you were before. That was sixteen years ago. You were young, scared, pregnant, and desperate, and disempowered by a loser of a dad. Now you're a smart, protective, financially secure mama bear who doesn't need anything from a man. That means you're in a position of power, so it's time to trust yourself and go live life."

Sofia let out her breath. "I want to, but this..." She tapped her fingers to her heart. "Is scared."

"I know. It's scary. But the man wore a prosthetic so he could come to your party. And he makes you glow. I think it's worth it."

Sofia took a breath, then asked the question that had been weighing on her. "What if he wants me only so that he can have Gabby? What if I'm the path to his daughter?"

"With the way he looks at you, there's no chance of that,"

Jocie said. "Sofia, you're an amazing woman. It's time you saw that, and trusted that your worth being loved by good people."

At that moment, Gabby and Keegan came back into the store, both of them laughing at something Gabby was telling him. It was such a sweet moment, the two of them together. Her heart turned over. "I want to hug him for accepting Gabby so completely."

"Then hug him. And then tackle him while you're at it." Jocie winked at her. "I'd tell you if I thought you were at risk with him, but I don't think you are." She gave her a quick hug. "Let's go finish up this party, and then you can figure out whether you want to date this old man or not."

She stepped away, waving her hands. "Okay, ladies and gents! It's time for the raffle giveaways! All proceeds go to the local women's shelter, as you all know. Sofia, it's prize time."

This was always her favorite part of the event. They got enough donations from local businesses and authors that they were able to put together fifty raffle baskets, which meant that most people got them. The joy people had when their name was called was infectious, ending the night on a high note. "Gabby and Kevin? Do you guys want to deliver the baskets?"

Both of her favorite humans said yes, and Sofia smiled as they made their way up to the front. Little Millie was sleeping on a chair by the fire, leaving them free to deliver happiness to the people she loved.

As she fished the first raffle slip out of the jar, her gaze slid to Keegan. He was watching her, and flashed her a grin that made her insides turn over. What would happen when everyone left? Would Keegan leave? Did she want him to? Or did she want to invite him into her sanctuary?

She didn't know.

CHAPTER TWENTY-SEVEN

AN HOUR LATER, Sofia stood in the door of her store, watching as Keegan and Gabby drove off for ice cream. Everyone had left, including Jocie. The store was cleaned up. The party over for another year.

Keegan had invited her to join him and Gabby for ice cream, but Sofia had declined.

She wanted Gabby to have her own relationship with Keegan, so her daughter would be secure with him no matter what happened between the adults.

But watching them drive away created such intense longing in Sofia that she almost ran out the door after them to flag them down.

Could they really be a family? A trio? Her longing surprised her, and worried her. Did she want a family and a dad for Gabby so much that she was willing to be lured into Keegan's circle, just so she could have the life she'd never had? Maybe she wasn't as independent as she'd thought, which meant that maybe she'd fallen for him for the wrong reasons.

She let out her breath. "How do I know if I can trust how I feel about you, Keegan?"

There was no answer in the crisp night air, and once his taillights were out of sight, there was no point in standing outside.

She walked back inside and shut and locked the store door, then leaned against it. Was she going to invite him to stay over when he got back? If she could trust him with her daughter, then couldn't she trust him with herself? Theoretically, yes. Right?

So, what was holding her back?

Wimpiness? Self-punishment? Martyrdom? Or some sixth sense that she couldn't put her finger on? Or maybe her lack of trust in herself.

The store felt empty and quiet, and she missed Gabby. She missed Keegan.

No. She didn't want to feel sad or despondent. Empowered, enlightened decisions were never made from a position of feeling lonely.

So, she shut out the melancholy, and looked around the store. The embers in the fireplace were fading, but the Christmas lights were still sparkling on the walls and the tree. She smiled, remembering the feel of the party. The camaraderie. The love.

She'd created that. She and Jocie. With love, commitment, and consistency over the years. It had been a labor of love from the start, and she'd cherished every minute of it.

She let herself feel pride in what she'd created. In the world she'd built. In the daughter she'd raised. She let herself be proud of herself, and see what she'd done and who she was.

As she stood there, she noticed the beautiful bookcases that she'd acquired. The assortment of antique chairs and loveseats that warmed the store, furniture she'd picked up at garage sales and antique shops, so that she could create a store that people wanted to hang out in. She smiled at the tall plant in the corner that had been a tiny sprig when she'd started. Now it reached almost to the celling. The signed books behind glass, one for every author who had come to the store for an event. There were hundreds now, because her store had become a regular stop on many book tours.

She'd done amazing things here. Without her Harvard degree. Without a man to lean on. Without her mom to support her.

Suddenly, she realized that in all her work, she'd forgotten to ever feel good about who she was and what she'd done.

Jocie was right.

She wasn't the scared, disempowered, alone nineteen-year-old, so desperate that she'd take any handout.

She *was* a powerful, badass chick. She grinned, suddenly feeling lighter than she had in a long time. Of course she could trust herself. *Of course she could.*

And she wanted Keegan. With all her heart. For herself. For Gabby. She had no idea how to work out the geographical issues, but she was willing to be open about it, because she knew now, that she'd never give up who she was for a man.

Not again.

Not ever.

And Keegan, with his prosthetic nose, wasn't the type to ask her to.

She let out a breath, elation filling her heart. She knew what she wanted, and she was going to try! And she wanted to start right now! Who knew? Maybe she'd open a second bookstore in Bend, and build a second community to support the one she and Jocie had running so smoothly now.

Her heart dancing, she broke into a run and raced for the stairs, to grab the car keys to the rental that Keegan had secured for her until her car was fixed.

She bounced up the stairs two at a time, raced down the hall, and flung her bedroom door open.

Sitting on her bed, pointing a gun at her, was the man she'd been hiding from for sixteen years.

CHAPTER TWENTY-EIGHT

"I HAVE TO ASK YOU SOMETHING," Gabby said as she sat down at the picnic table across from Keegan with her ice cream.

"You bet." Keegan couldn't believe how at peace he was. He'd always figured himself to be a pretty happy dude, but the last forty-eight hours with Gabby and Sofia had been mind-blowing.

He'd found his place. He knew he had. He loved every second of being with them. He wished that Sofia had come with them, but he understood why she'd wanted them to have one-on-one time. Gabby needed to feel secure with him, regardless of Sofia, and he was doing his best to make her feel that way.

As he sat there across from Gabby, he was stunned with how lucky he was. This smart, sassy, amazing kid was his *daughter.* "But first, can I say something?"

She raised her brows. "Sure."

"I want to tell you how glad I am that you found me."

Her face brightened. "Really?"

"Absolutely." He leaned forward. "Gabby, I feel like I'm

the luckiest guy alive, that out of the blue, I've got this incredible young woman who is my daughter. I always wanted kids, but it didn't seem like that was happening, then you showed up in my life. I will always be grateful as hell that you tracked me down."

Her smile widened. "All right."

All right. Two simple, non-committal words from a teenager that were filled with joy, relief, and emotion.

"I've never been a dad before," he said. "So, we're going to have to figure it out as we go."

She looked down at her ice cream. "Well, I've never had a dad before, so I don't know how it works either."

His heart turned over at her soft confession. "Do you play sports? An instrument? Sing? Act in plays?"

She looked up. "I play three sports. Field hockey in the fall, I swim in the winter, and I play lacrosse in the spring. Why?"

"I'll come to your games and your meets. Can you text me your schedule?"

She stared at him. "You want to come to my games?"

"Hell, yeah." He paused. "Is that okay?"

"But you can't be seen around me."

He shrugged. "I'm hoping we can address that situation, but in the meantime, I paid enough money for this makeup that I'm sure she'd be willing to do it again."

"You'd wear that makeup again so you can come to my games?"

"Sure. I'll be Grandpa Kevin if I have to."

"But you live in Oregon."

He felt her doubt that she could be enough that he'd want to really come to her games and meets. That meeting and having an outing was one thing, but to come to games was something else. That was too regular, too much like the dad who had never shown up for her. "I have a bunch of cars I like to drive, plus two private jets. We're also researching getting a helicopter. So, getting to your games isn't going to be a problem."

"But you have a job."

"I own the business. The boss will never fire me for taking time off to go to my daughter's games. Plus, I'm thinking of stepping away from the business side and refocusing on the baking and cultivating local relationships with our mom-and-pop customer base. So, I don't need to be at the offices as much."

"But..." Gabby was running out of objections, but he allowed her to take her time. He knew how difficult it was to trust. "But your family is in Oregon. You can't leave them."

"My family is in Oregon," he agreed. "But my family is also in Washington. Sitting at this table with me, actually. So, going back and forth isn't a hardship. It's automatic. I wouldn't have it any other way."

Gabby stared at him, then suddenly, she leapt up, ran around the table, and flung herself into his arms.

He caught her and held tight, burying his face in her hair as she clung to him. He could feel her trembling, and he could hear her muffled sobs.

"Gabby?" he whispered. "I wouldn't be alive today if my Hart family hadn't been there for me. I know how important family is, how much you need to be able to count on them, no matter how they come into your life. You're that to me now. You will *always* be able to count on me, and I will *never* let you down."

She clung tighter to him, her face buried in his chest.

His throat tightened. God, the chance to be a dad? To be *her* dad? What a gift. "I love you, Gabby. You can count on that."

"I love you, too, Keegan," she whispered, her voice muffled against his shirt.

Suddenly, his eyes filled, and he couldn't respond. He closed his eyes and held tight to this magical being that was his daughter, who had welcomed him into her life.

It took more than a few moments before Gabby finally pulled back, her eyes red, her cheeks stained with tears. "You're such a jerk for making me cry."

He laughed softly. "If I do the dad thing right, I'll probably have to piss you off a lot. I hear that's part of the deal."

"I know." She rolled her eyes as she retreated to her side of the table. She grabbed a napkin and blew her nose and wiped her cheeks, then tossed it to the side. "I'm going to tell you now that since stealing my mom's car worked out so well, I'll probably need to steal yours too. Yours are nicer than hers was."

He picked up his coffee. "Well, then, you should know that I'm not going to bribe you for your love. That includes things like, not letting you take my vehicles without permission. Or giving you a credit card with unlimited spending."

Her face brightened. "But you'll give me one with limited spending? Like what? Twenty thousand dollars a month? Because I feel like that's just a drop in the bucket for you, and I'm totally worth it."

He laughed. "I'm not giving you a cent without your mom's permission. She's been making the rules for sixteen years, and I'm going to respect them."

Gabby wrinkled her nose. "That's so annoying. She's such a stick in the mud."

"Is she?" He grinned. "Seems to me she's a pretty amazing, bold, happening woman who can rock any room she steps into."

Gabby's brows shot up. "Are you going to marry her, then?"

He choked on his coffee. "Marry her?"

"Yeah. I mean, you wore a fake nose for her. I feel like

that's making a statement. Or are you going to break her heart? Because I'll be honest, that would piss me off on a thousand levels if you made her cry."

Damn. He loved the loyalty between Gabby and Sofia. They had a brilliant relationship. "I don't know how it's going to work out," he said honestly. "And I hope like hell I never make her cry."

"Do you love her?"

He sat back, contemplating how honest to be. Finally, he decided on the truth. This was his daughter, and he wanted to set the foundation of honesty in their relationship. "I do."

Gabby leaned forward, studying his face. "Like really love her? Like *love* love?"

He met her gaze without hesitating. "I do. I loved her when we first met, and I still do. I love her differently now, but it's far more powerful."

Gabby pursed her lips. "I think she loves you. The way she looks at you...she's glowing."

A rush of emotion flooded Keegan. "I hope so."

"So, would you *like* to marry her?"

He laughed. "I think that she's the first person I would need to tell that to."

She grinned. "So, that's a yes. Damn! That's so cool. If you marry her, though, you can't try to take over our lives."

Ah...like mother, like daughter. "If I were to marry your mom, we would all decide together how we want to create a life together. That's what family is."

She cocked her head. "Okay."

Okay. Just like that. Accepting him. "I appreciate your trust in me. I won't let you down."

"I almost hope you do. Then we could sue you for billions." The twinkle in Gabby's eyes told him she was kidding, and he laughed.

"My billions are all yours, remember? I asked Eliana to put that together for you."

"Yeah, about that." She frowned at him. "Why can't you keep us safe?"

"I'm working on that with my brothers. We're powerful with deep resources. We plan to find a way."

Her face lit up and she grinned. "You're such a badass. I love that. I had no idea. I thought you were all a bunch of useless richies."

"Useless? I'm sure my siblings will be thrilled to hear that."

"Oh, my God! Don't tell them!" Gabby slapped his forearm. "I'll disown you as my dad."

"Too late. It's out there. You're stuck with me."

"I'm not stuck with you."

"You are." Damn, he liked saying that. "But—" He felt his phone buzzing in his pocket. Instinctively, he pulled it out, as he always did. The Harts always took calls from each other, no matter what was happening. He frowned when he saw the name. "It's Eliana." He answered the phone. "What's up?"

"Are Gabby and Sofia with you?"

Alarm shot through him at her tone. "Gabby is. Why?" He gestured to Gabby to get up and pointed to his truck. Her eyes widened, and together, they ran toward his truck, ice cream forgotten.

"He's found her. He landed in Seattle a few hours ago. I just called Sofia, but she's not answering her phone. I texted her the code that he'd found her, and she didn't respond. She has to respond. That's our plan. If she's not responding, either she doesn't have her phone on her, or she can't text back."

Fear shot through him. "Fuck. We're on the way. Send the cops."

"On it." She hung up.

"The cops? Why?" Gabby was already in the front seat, fastening her seat belt.

Keegan held up his hand to ask for a moment, then called the security team he'd left in front of the store.

They didn't answer.

Swearing, he called Brody. "Get people to Sofia's house now!"

"Keegan! What's going on?" Gabby's face paled. "Did he find her? Is my mom in trouble?" The look of stark terror on her face was like a stab to his gut.

"I gotta go, Brody. Get people there now." He hung up and focused on the teenager beside him. "We're going to get to her in time, Gabby."

"He's found her?" Tears filled her eyes. "Hurry! Please hurry!"

He stopped trying to reassure her and hit the gas.

CHAPTER TWENTY-NINE

SOFIA FROZE, paralyzed by the sight of the man who had haunted her for so long.

Sitting there.

On her bed.

In her room.

Wearing a custom suit, polished shoes, and a watch that cost more than the building they were in. Money. Connections. Power. All the things that controlled her life before, he still had.

He didn't smile. "Imagine my surprise when one of my investigators told me that you were alive and sleeping with Keegan Hart."

She fought to think, to think clearly, not to panic. The last time she'd seen him, she'd been scared, young, and vulnerable. But she'd had fifteen years to become the woman who was ready for this moment.

"You didn't die," he said. "I suspected as much when they didn't find either of your bodies and a chunk of my money was gone. But you were hard to find. So very difficult."

His eyes were dark and cold. His voice hard and uncaring. His tone smug and arrogant.

How had she worried that Keegan might be like him? That she wouldn't be able to trust her judgment that Keegan was safe? Now that she was in front of the man who had haunted her for so long, it was so obvious to her what a monster he was. She'd never make that mistake again.

The realization was such a relief. She could trust herself. She could trust how she felt about Keegan.

"You're smiling? You think it's funny that you faked your death and hid from me?" He rose to his feet, slow and menacing. But he wasn't as big as she remembered. Not as tall. Not as muscled.

Anger rushed through her. Anger that he'd made her a victim. Anger that she'd let him take her life from her. Anger that she'd been afraid for so long.

Now that the moment was here, it felt so old. Like she'd relived it a thousand times already. Gabby wasn't home, so he couldn't get her. Gabby had a dad and a family, so if anything happened to Sofia, her daughter would be okay. So, the fear of being killed and leaving her daughter alone and unprotected slid away, leaving behind the woman who was done with being a victim.

He pointed the gun at her and moved toward her. "A gun is too easy for you. You'll suffer, and then I'll find your daughter---"

"You won't find her. You won't be able to hurt her. She's protected now." It felt so good and empowering to say that, to know it was true. She began to inch toward her nightstand, toward the gun she kept in there. "You don't get to have her."

"I can get to anyone." He watched her move. "I found your gun. You think I'm that stupid?"

She stopped. "You are stupid, yes. I do think that," she

said, goading him. She'd never goaded him before. She'd sat quietly and tried not to piss him off, which had empowered the bully. But she didn't want to sit quietly anymore. She'd come too far, and it wasn't until this moment, facing him that she truly understood how far she had come over the last decade and a half.

He cursed at her and lunged at her, but she saw him coming and dove to the side, toward the nightstand. She grabbed the cord of the lamp as she dove, yanked it off the nightstand and swung the lamp by the cord as hard as she could.

It crashed into the side of his head and shattered as he dropped.

She grabbed his gun and bolted for the door, then paused in the threshold, turning back to look at him.

He was motionless on the floor, a lump of man on her carpet.

She stopped and stared at him, letting her breathe in the fact she'd beaten him. She knew it was because he hadn't expected her to fight back, and he hadn't been prepared. Next time, she wouldn't get him, but right now, she felt powerful and strong, a woman who could choose her life and choose her future.

His fingers started to move, and she stepped back. She raised the gun and pointed it at him, but she didn't want to shoot him. She didn't want to have to be that person.

The front door slammed. "Mom! Mom!"

Then Keegan's voice rang out. "Sofia! Where are you?"

Relief rushed through her. "Upstairs! In my room. I'm okay!"

Feet thundered on the stairs, but by the time Keegan appeared at the top of the steps, the man she'd feared for so long had made it to his hands and knees. "You little—"

Keegan reached her, and she handed him the gun. "You can finish it."

Keegan grabbed the gun and aimed it into her bedroom. "Get down," he snapped. "Now."

As the monster she'd feared for so long dropped back down at the sight of Keegan with the gun, Sofia grabbed Gabby and pulled her back from the door, so she didn't have to look inside. "Hey, baby, Keegan's got it."

"He's here?" Gabby looked terrified, and Sofia realized she'd done that to her daughter, made her terrified of a nameless, faceless ghost.

It was time to disempower what she'd created. "Come see." She put her arm around Gabby and led her to the bedroom. They walked to the doorway and peered inside. Keegan was on the phone, and her ex-husband was face-down on the carpet, blood oozing from the side of his head.

"Did you kill him?" Gabby whispered.

"No. I didn't need to."

Keegan didn't take his gaze off his target. "Sofia? Are you all right?"

"I'm perfect. And I love you."

He grinned. "You can't tell me that when I can't even look at you, let alone tackle you and shower you with love."

"I can do whatever I want, actually. And I want to love you. And I want to figure out how to make this work without either of us giving up what we love."

Gabby squealed and hugged her. "I totally thought you were going to dump Keegan."

Sofia laughed, feeling so liberated and free. With Keegan handling the gun, and her own new power, the fear was gone. "I thought about it, but he's just so rich, I thought it was silly."

Keegan grunted. "As soon as I don't have to hold this jerk

at gunpoint, I'm going to have to clarify that thinking. You get my money anyway."

"I know. So, I guess I love you just because I love you." It felt so good to say the words, to feel the words, to allow the emotions to fill her.

"Me, too," Gabby said. "He told me he loves both of us."

"I do," Keegan said. "But I really think there's a better time and place for this kind of talk." He waggled the gun at her ex. "Keep your head on the floor. Don't move, or I'll happily shoot you for terrorizing the women I love all this time."

"And there's one more thing," Sofia said.

"What's that?"

"You remember that thing you wanted to do with Gabby's birth certificate? Well, it's okay with me."

Keegan's gaze shot to hers this time, a look of absolute love on his face. "Really?"

Her heart turned over at the joy on his face. This man. *This man*. God, she loved him.

"What?" Gabby tugged on her arm. "What about my birth certificate?"

Sofia grinned. "You can tell her."

Keegan was smiling now as he kept his gaze on his prisoner. "I'm not sure this is the best timing."

"The timing is perfect. No more delays, Keegan. No more wasted moments in our lives."

"What are you guys talking about?" Gabby asked again.

Keegan's smile widened. "Gabby, if it's okay with you, your mom and I are going to amend your birth certificate to put my name as your dad. Since I am."

Gabby's eyes filled with tears. "Really?"

He nodded. "Really."

Sofia smiled. "Yes. No more blank line on there."

Gabby threw her arms around Sofia's waist and buried her

face in her chest. Sofia hugged her and exchanged smiles with Keegan. The expression on his face was pure love, and she held out her arm to him.

He sighed melodramatically. "See? Not perfect timing. I want to be in that hug fest right now."

"Guns are snuggly," Sofia said. "It's almost the same."

"I agree." Gabby turned to face him, her head resting on Sofia's shoulder. "You really want to do that, Keegan?"

He nodded. "Absolutely. Your last name is Navarro, but you're also a Hart, and the whole world will know it now."

Sofia's throat clogged with emotion, and Gabby's arms tightened around Sofia. "Do I get a trust fund?"

"How about several? One for each day of the week?"

She grinned. "Perfect. And cars?"

"Never. You don't get to drive ever again, according to your mom."

"Mom," Gabby wailed in protest, but her eyes were dancing.

At that moment, Sofia heard sirens pull up in front of the building, and she relaxed even more. Within a few minutes, the police had swarmed the room and taken over.

Sofia and Gabby retreated to the hall, and a few minutes later, Keegan walked out.

Her heart filled as he headed toward them, his arms out to sweep them both into a massive hug. "I love both of you like crazy," he said as they melted into a big pile of hugs. "Thank God you finally caved in to my charm, Sofia. I wasn't sure how much longer I was going to be able to last giving you space."

She laughed and kissed him, even as he had one arm around Gabby. "You lasted just long enough."

"I guess I did." He kissed her back, long, intimate, and delicious, until Gabby finally poked them.

"You guys have to stop! That's so uncool!"

Sofia laughed and pulled back, well aware of the happiness in Gabby's voice even as she protested.

She met Keegan's gaze, and her heart filled when she saw the pure joy and love in his eyes.

It might have taken sixteen years, but they'd finally found their way to each other.

"Merry Christmas, ladies," Keegan said. "We're home."

≈

WANT MORE HARTS? *A Rogue Cowboy Finds Love* will be available soon!

If you enjoyed this Christmas romance, check out these feel-good holiday romances by Stephanie:

A Real Cowboy for Christmas
A Real Cowboy for the Holidays
Wrapped Up in You

New to Stephanie's cowboy world, and want more heart-melting cowboys? If so, you *have* to try my *Wyoming Rebels* series about nine cowboy brothers who find love in the most romantic, most heartwarming, most sigh-worthy ways you can imagine. Get started with *A Real Cowboy Never Says No* right now. You will be sooo glad you did, I promise!

If you want more small-town, emotional feel-good romances like the *Hart Ranch Billionaires*, you'd love my *Birch Crossing* series! Get started with *Unexpectedly Mine* today!

Are you in the mood for some feel-good, cozy mystery fun that's chock full of murder, mayhem, and women you'll wish were your best friends? If so, you'll fall in love with *Double Twist!*

Are you a fan of magic, love, and laughter? If so, dive

into my paranormal romantic comedy *Immortally Sexy* series, starting with the first book, *To Date an Immortal*.

Is dark, steamy paranormal romance your jam? If so, definitely try my award-winning *Order of the Blade* series, starting with book one, *Darkness Awakened.*

SNEAK PEEK: A REAL COWBOY FOR THE HOLIDAYS

EMMA SPUN AROUND AND started to sprint across the Rollins Tree Farm parking lot to the store, and immediately ran smack into the side of a truck that had just pulled in.

She stumbled back, falling on her butt, as the pickup truck hit the brakes. God, she was such an idiot!

The driver jumped out and ran around the front of the truck. "Are you all right?"

Emma recognized his voice immediately. Quintin Stockton, the man she'd just been thinking about. She looked up, and her heart literally did a little flutter at the sight of him. He'd been a rebellious troublemaker when they were in high school, but now he was all man now. Tall, muscular, and strong-jawed. His cowboy hat was tilted at a jaunty angle, hinting at the arrogance that she had once associated with him.

Nothing scary about him anymore. Just raw, heated testosterone that made every part of her start to hum.

She kinda wanted to gawk at him, but that would be insanely rude. She was sure he'd never recognize her after so many years, so she just gave him a brilliant smile. "I'm fine. Feeling a little disappointed that I'm not strong enough to run right through a pickup truck, but I'll get over it."

His eyebrows shot up. "Nerd Girl?"

Nerd Girl. She'd forgotten the names they had for each other, back when he'd been a grumpy rebel and she'd been the overly responsible daughter-of-the-owner trying to get him to work. She grinned. "Yep. Rebel Boy, I presume?"

He still had a roguish look to him that was impossible to pin down. It was his eyes, she decided. They were the eyes of someone who would flat out refuse to play by any rules, unless he made him.

As a teenager, that had scared her.

Now? That made him deliciously attractive. She had grown to hate rules.

A smile quirked at the corner of Quintin's mouth as he held out his hand to help her up. "Rebel Boy. I forgot about that." His voice was deeper now, a richer timbre that was stunningly masculine.

She'd never thought of him as dateable material. He'd just been the irritating teenager who'd made her life a little crazy...and a lot more interesting. But only as friends. Co-workers. Co-conspirators, maybe.

But now? She couldn't stop thinking about him as a man, which was a little shocking, given that she'd been completely shut down from men for six years.

Quintin didn't appear to be looking at her as if he wanted to strip her naked, so she plastered on a friendly, neutral smile. "Well, I forgot about Nerd Girl, so we're even." She took his proffered hand, surprised by how warm it was against her freezing ones. "Didn't you run me over with the golf cart once?"

His brows shot up, and his smile widened. "I bumped you. I didn't run you over, and I felt like shit about it for years."

She laughed. "Years? Really? Because of my tiny thigh bruise?"

"It was a nice thigh. It deserved better." He helped her to her feet. His dark brown eyes searched hers with genuine concern. "You sure you're not hurt?"

His protectiveness wrapped around her like a warm, well-muscled hug. "No, I'm good." She brushed the snow off her butt and tried to pretend that she hadn't noticed the broad expanse of his chest or the whiskers on his jaw. "What can I do for you?"

A ridiculous part of her sort of fantasized that the answer would involve things that a responsible, single mom should never do with a rebellious troublemaker....

Which was both shocking and amazing...and unrealistic, of course.

But to even have that brief fantasy?

A good sign that her soul was still fighting to live.

What happens when Quintin offers to help out at the tree farm for the Christmas season? Don't miss this steamy, magical holiday romance! One-click your copy of *A Real Cowboy for the Holidays* right now so you don't forget!

SNEAK PEEK: UNEXPECTEDLY MINE

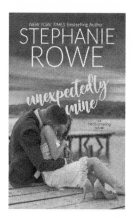

"This book wove...deep inside my heart and soul."
-Amy W (Amazon Review)

Single mom Clare is too busy for love...until a single dad rents her spare room and teaches her how to trust again.

CLARE WAS LIFTING the box of cupcakes off the front counter when she became aware of the utter silence of the general store. Even at the funerals of her parents, she hadn't heard this kind of silence in Birch Crossing.

Awareness prickled down her arms, and she looked at Norm, who was in his usual spot behind the front register. She could have sworn that there was amusement crinkling his gray eyes when he nodded toward something behind her.

Clare spun around, and there he was.

Griffin Friesé.

Her mystical knight in shining armor from last night.

Her heart began to race as she met his gaze. His stare was intense, penetrating all the way to her core. She was yanked back to that moment of his hands on her hips, of his strength as he'd lifted her. The power in his body as he'd emerged from his truck during the thundering rain and raging wind. Her body began to thrum, and his expression grew hooded, his eyes never leaving hers, as if he were trying to memorize every feature on her face.

He was wearing a heavy leather jacket that flanked strong thighs and broad shoulders. His eyes were dark, as dark as they'd been last night in the storm. Whiskers shadowed his jaw, giving him a rough and untamed look. His boots were still caked with mud, but his jeans were pressed and clean. His light blue dress shirt was open at the collar, revealing a hint of skin and the flash of a thin gold chain at his throat. His hair was short and perfectly gelled, not messy and untamed like it had been last night. A heavy gold watch sat captive on the strong wrist that had supported her so easily.

Today, he wasn't the dark and rugged hero of last night.

Well, okay, he still was. His power transcended mud, storms, nice watches, and dress shirts.

But he was also, quite clearly and quite ominously, an

outsider, a man who did not fit into the rural Maine town of Birch Crossing.

Then he smiled, a beautiful, tremendous smile with a dimple in his right cheek. "How's your daughter?"

A dimple? He had a dimple? Clare hadn't noticed the dimple last night. It made him look softer, more human, more approachable, almost endearing. Suddenly all her trepidation vanished, replaced by a feeling of giddiness and delight to see him. She smiled back. "She's still asleep, but she's okay. Thanks for your help last night rescuing her."

"My pleasure." His smile faded, and a speculative gleam came into his dark eyes. "And how are you?"

No longer feeling like a total wreck, that was for sure. Not with Griffin Friesé studying her as if she were the only thing he ever wanted to look at again. Dear God, the way he was looking at her made her want to drop the cupcakes and her clothes, and saunter with decadent sensuality across the floor toward him, his stare igniting every cell in her body. "I'm fine." She swallowed, horrified by how throaty her voice sounded. "Thank you," she said. "I owe you."

"No, you owe me nothing." He smiled again, a softness to his face that made her heart turn over. "Seeing you hug Katie was plenty."

"Oh, dear Lord," Eppie muttered behind her. "Now he's going to kill Katie, too."

Clare stiffened and jerked her gaze from Griffin. The entire store was watching them in rapt silence, listening to every word. Oh, God. How had she forgotten where they were? Wright & Sons was the epicenter of gossip in Birch Crossing, and everyone had just witnessed her gaping at this handsome stranger.

Assuming her decades-old role as Clare's self-appointed protector, Eppie had folded her arms and was trying to crush Griffin with her glare, for daring to tempt Clare.

Astrid and Emma were leaning against the doorjamb, huge grins on their faces, clearly supportive of any opportunity to pry Clare out of her dateless life of isolation. But Norm's eyes were narrowed, and Ophelia was letting some scrambled eggs burn while she gawked at them. Everyone was waiting to see how Clare was going to respond to him.

Oh, man. What was she doing nearly throwing herself at him? In front of everyone? She quickly took a step back and cleared her throat.

Griffin's eyebrows shot up at her retreat, then his eyes narrowed. "Kill off Katie, *too*? " He looked right at Eppie. "Who else am I going to kill?"

Eppie lifted her chin and turned her head, giving him a view of the back of her hot pink hat.

"The rumors claim that you're in town to murder your ex-wife and daughter," Astrid volunteered cheerfully. "But don't worry. Not all of us believe them."

"My daughter?" Pain flashed across Griffin's face, a stark anguish so real that Clare felt her out heart tighten. Just as quickly, the vulnerability disappeared from his face, replaced by a hard, cool expression.

But she'd seen it. She'd seen his pain, pain he clearly kept hidden, just as she suppressed her own. Suddenly, she felt terrible about the rumors. How could she have listened to rumors about him when he was clearly struggling with pain, some kind of trauma with regard to his daughter?

She realized he was watching her, as if he were waiting for something. For what? To see if she believed the rumors?

She glanced around and saw the entire store was waiting for her response. Eppie gave her a solemn nod, encouraging her to stand up and condemn this handsome stranger who'd saved Clare's daughter. Sudden anger surged inside her. "Oh, come on," she blurted out. "You can't really believe he's a murderer?"

Astrid grinned, Eppie shook her head in dismay, and the rest of the room was silent.

No one else jumped in to help her defend Griffin, and suddenly Clare felt very exposed, as if everyone in the room could see exactly how deeply she'd been affected by him last night. How she'd lain awake all night, thinking of his hands on her hips, of the way his deep voice had wrapped around her, of how he'd made her yearn for the touch of a man for the first time in a very long time.

Heat burned her cheeks, and she glanced uncomfortably at Griffin, wondering if he was aware of her reaction to him. To her surprise, his face had cooled, devoid of that warmth that they'd initially shared, clearly interpreting her silence as a capitulation to the rumors.

He narrowed his eyes, then turned away, ending their conversation.

Regret rushed through Clare as she glanced at Astrid, torn between wanting to call him back, and gratefully grasping the freedom his rejection had given her, freedom from feelings and desires that she didn't have time to deal with.

"I need a place to stay," Griffin said. "A place without rats, preferably."

Griffin's low request echoed through the room, and Clare spun around in shock. Then she saw he was directing his question to Norm, not to her. Relief rushed through her, along with a stab of disappointment.

No, it was good he wasn't asking to stay at her place. Yes, she owed him, on a level beyond words, but she couldn't afford to get involved with him, for too many reasons. Staying at her house would be putting temptation where she couldn't afford it. There was *no way* she was going to offer up her place, even though her renter had just vacated, leaving her with an unpleasant gap in her income stream.

"Griffin stayed at the Dark Pines Motel last night," Judith whispered, just loudly enough for the whole store to hear.

"Really?" Guilt washed through Clare. The Dark Pines Motel was quite possibly the most unkempt and disgusting motel in the entire state of Maine. How had he ended up there?

"Well, now, Griffin," Norm said, as he tipped his chair back and let it tap against the unfinished wall. "Most places won't open for another month when the summer folk start to arrive. And the Black Loon Inn is booked for the Smith-Pineal wedding for the next week. It's Dark Pines or nothing."

Griffin frowned. "There has to be something. A bed and breakfast?"

Norm shook his head. "Not this time of year, but I probably have some rat traps in the back I could loan you for your stay.'

"Rat traps?" Griffin echoed. "That's my best option?"

Astrid grinned at Clare, a sparkle in her eyes that made Clare's stomach leap with alarm. She grabbed Astrid's arm. " Don't you dare—"

"Clare's renter just moved out," Astrid announced, her voice ringing out in the store. "Griffin can stay in her spare room. No rats, and it comes with free Wi-Fi. Best deal in town."

Oh, dear *God.* Clare's whole body flamed hot, and she whipped around. *Please tell me he didn't hear that.*

But Griffin was staring right at her.

Of course he'd heard. And so had everyone else.

Like it? Get it now!

BOOKS BY STEPHANIE ROWE

MYSTERY

MIA MURPHY SERIES
(COZY MYSTERY)
Double Twist
Top Notch
Gone Rogue

CONTEMPORARY ROMANCE

WYOMING REBELS SERIES
(CONTEMPORARY WESTERN ROMANCE)
A Real Cowboy Never Says No
A Real Cowboy Knows How to Kiss
A Real Cowboy Rides a Motorcycle
A Real Cowboy Never Walks Away
A Real Cowboy Loves Forever
A Real Cowboy for Christmas
A Real Cowboy Always Trusts His Heart
A Real Cowboy Always Protects

PARANORMAL

ORDER OF THE BLADE SERIES
(PARANORMAL ROMANCE)
Darkness Awakened
Darkness Seduced
Darkness Surrendered
Forever in Darkness
Darkness Reborn
Darkness Arisen
Darkness Unleashed
Inferno of Darkness
Darkness Possessed
Shadows of Darkness
Hunt the Darkness
Darkness Awakened: Reimagined

IMMORTALLY DATING SERIES
(FUNNY PARANORMAL ROMANCE)
To Date an Immortal
To Date a Dragon
Devilishly Dating
To Kiss a Demon

HEART OF THE SHIFTER SERIES
(PARANORMAL ROMANCE)
Dark Wolf Rising
Dark Wolf Unbound

STANDALONE PARANORMAL ROMANCE
Leopard's Kiss
Not Quite Dead

FUNNY URBAN FANTASY

BOOKS BY STEPHANIE ROWE

Guardian of Magic
The Demon You Trust

DEVILISHLY SEXY SERIES
(FUNNY PARANORMAL ROMANCE)
Not Quite a Devil

ROMANTIC SUSPENSE

ALASKA HEAT SERIES
(ROMANTIC SUSPENSE)
Ice
Chill
Ghost
Burn
Hunt (novella)

BOXED SETS

Order of the Blade (Books 1-4)
Protectors of the Heart (A Six-Book First-in-Series Collection)
Wyoming Rebels Boxed Set (Books 1-3)

For a complete list of Stephanie's books, click here.

A QUICK FAVOR

Did you enjoy Keegan and Sofia's story?

People are often hesitant to try new books or new authors. A few reviews can encourage them to make that leap and give it a try. If you enjoyed *A Rogue Cowboy's Christmas Surprise* and think others will as well, please consider taking a moment and writing one or two sentences *on the etailer and/or Goodreads* to help this story find the readers who would enjoy it. Even the short reviews really make an impact!

Thank you a million times for reading my books! I love writing for you and sharing the journeys of these beautiful characters with you. I hope you find inspiration from their stories in your own life!

Love,
Stephanie

ABOUT THE AUTHOR

New York Times and USA Today bestselling author Stephanie Rowe is the author of more than sixty published novels. Notably, she is a Vivian® Award nominee, a RITA® Award winner and a five-time nominee, and a Golden Heart® Award winner and two-time nominee. She loves her puppies, tennis, and trying to live her best, truest life. For info on Stephanie's newest releases, join her newsletter today!

Sign me up for Stephanie Newsletter

www.stephanierowe.com